# The Je...

## revenge

By Simon Wilson

# *Forward*

This book has been written because of my wife. She told me that I needed to better myself, so in my mid-thirties I took GCSE English. Whilst doing it I discovered that I really enjoyed the story writing element. So, after I passed the exam, I decided that I would take a story writing course and asked my English teacher if they were any good and he told me, if you want to write, just write. So I went off and did just that. Well sort of. I actually didn't write anything for ages until the story you see here which literally just popped into my head. Not sure where it came from, I'd probably just been watching a well-known film franchise about pirates or a certain T.V. series about the same thing. Whatever the case, in it popped and I just wrote it with no planning, just a general idea of where it was going and who was going to be in it. The research was really good fun and I learned a lot about pirates and their way of life. In fact, all of the pirates in this book are real! Each of them has a story of their own written in history. I may have moved them around in time a little bit here and there to suit my own purposes, but that's artistic license for you! I hope that you enjoy reading this book as much as I have enjoyed writing it, and with that, I present to you,

## *The Jenny's Revenge*

# Chapter one.

Jenny: A name or term used by pirates and sailors to describe a prostitute.

As Anne lay in the mud and filth behind the Cabin boy, one of Port Royal's smaller but still popular taverns come brothel, she wondered how it had all gone so terribly wrong. She had always considered herself to be a good judge of character, able to spot and steer clear from those of a mind to hurt her or not pay for services rendered. This latest Tom had been different. He looked well kept, almost clean and mostly sober with an innocent looking face that was baby like in its appearance. At the time Anne had considered that he looked quite naïve compared to most of the patronage that frequented the Cabin boy. She quickly checked her appearance ensuring that a suitable amount of her ample breasts were on show and her mousy brown hair tumbled down her front to frame them. Then she approached him, looking up at him with doe brown eyes, saying all the usual words of a women in her line of work, and when he looked interested in taking things further, offered to take him upstairs to one of the rooms so that they could come to an accord over price and do business. It was at that point that the Tom had gotten panicked and said he needed air. As Anne watched him leave the tavern, she couldn't help but to feel a bit sorry for him, deciding that it must be his first time. That being said, she didn't want to lose his patronage so quickly followed him out into the night air. In another lifetime Anne rather fancied that she could have been an actress in one of those fancy stage shows. She and many of the other girls in her line of work often had to play a role in order to secure some coin. The sad truth was that it was often the best way to get through many of the vulgar things her clients wanted to do. It was a lot easier after all if you could say it was happening to somebody else instead of you. For this particular Tom she decided to use a motherly approach with lots of reassurance.

"What's the matter love?" she asked using the same tone of voice many mothers did when a child was crying.

"Don't be embarrassed. We all 'ad a first time. You come upstairs with me and I'll make it real special for you."

As she spoke Anne cozied up to the man, she was shorter than most and tiny compared to him. Trying to win him over by pressing her breasts against him and gazing wantonly up at him with her hazel eyes. As she did so she could feel a real tension in him, the muscles in his arms and back were taught as a Hawser line at high tide. Though his next words made her think she'd won him over she was soon to discover that she had made a terrible mistake.

"You sound just like my mother miss" he said taking Anne's arm in his hand.

"I hated my mother."

Anne looked up into the Tom's eyes. The smooth baby like features that had first drawn her attention were now gone replaced with rage and hatred.

"I HATED MY MOTHER!" he screamed in her face.

Anne started to struggle, she knew she was in serious trouble and needed to get away, but his grip was vice like from many years at sea and he easily overpowered her. Looking around he saw the back ally where the tavern threw all of its rubbish and emptied its chamber pots. With a wicked grin he dragged Anne into its darkness.

"Come on missy. I'm gonna show you just what I did to my mother", his voice a low growl in the gloom. The last thing Anne could clearly remember was the man laughing, high pitched and childlike before darkness swallowed her.

Thankfully for Anne the human mind has a built-in defense mechanism that automatically blocks out traumatic events but as she came to it was evident that disgusting and violent acts had been heaped upon her. There was not an inch of Anne's body that did not hurt, inside and out.

The Tom's attack had been savage. She had been bitten in several places, her arms, her neck, her breasts, as if she had been attacked not by a man but by a wild animal. As if in sympathy for her plight the moon light that shone weakly into the ally now gave everything a soft edge, but Anne could still see that her clothing had been torn from her body. The light was also enough to show that the puddle she sat in came not from the contents of any chamber pot but instead flowed form between her legs, testament of the depravity of the man with a baby's face. She knew that she should be grateful that she had no recollection of the events that had befallen her, but she knew that his seemingly innocent features would haunt her for the rest of her days. Anne knew that she needed to move as sitting in the filth of the ally could, if it hadn't already, lead to infection. Her body though, would not obey her will so bad was the damaged bestowed upon it. She couldn't even muster the energy to weep or cry for help. Believing that all hope was lost and that she was to die lying in the mud and excrement of a whore house. A shadow fell upon her and through swollen eyes she could just make out several blurred outlines. Anne presumed that the Tom had returned, bringing a few of his ship mates to finish the job he had started but as she sank into merciful unconsciousness, she was pleasantly surprised to hear a soft voice telling her all would soon be right.

# Chapter two.

Tom: A name given to the patronage by prostitutes.

As Anne slowly regained consciousness she became aware of two things. First and foremost was that she was alive and secondly, but just as importantly, that she was in a rather comfortable cot instead of the filthy ally. She tried to open her eyes but discovered that after the beating she had received that one was fully swollen shut and the other opened only far enough to give a blurred image of her surroundings. She then decided to attempt sit up and improve her limited view, but her efforts were rewarded with a massive wave of pain and nausea. It was at this point that Anne considered changing her first assessment about being alive. She settled for a look around from the vantage point she had, moving only as far as she could with her head without passing out. Anne didn't know much about the inner workings of a ship or the outer when she thought about it, having only ever seen them in the harbor and then only at a distance. That being said, she could tell that she was aboard one now. When in harbour, a ship would constantly move with the tide causing its timbers to creak. Even on the calmest of days the wind could be heard whistling through the rigging and the sea would lap at the ships side. Fear gripped at Anne's heart, fear that the baby-faced Tom had somehow dragged her back to his ship to be used by the rest of his crew.

If that was the case, she reasoned with herself, why was she lying in a cot instead of strewn on the floor and why had, as far as she could feel, all her injuries been treated and dressed. A shadow appeared over her and the combination of the low light of the ship's interior mixed with her facial injuries rendered the person casting the shadow into little more than a distorted blur.

"This is it," Anne thought, "this is where the pain and abuse starts."

She started to sob, squeezed her eye shut and although she fought against it, having just rationalized there was no need for it, terror once again clawed at her. Terror of the unknown mixing with her memories of the ally.

"No need for that love".

At the sound of the voice Anne's sobbing stopped almost immediately. She recognized the voice as having been the one that had come from the alley behind the Cabin boy, but instead of a harsh male voice edged with violent intent, it was soft and feminine, filled with concern. Anne forced her eye to open as far as it could and although blurry through her tears and the swelling, could just make out the shape of the person who owned the voice. She was surprised to find that despite the attire and the various weapons that jutted out from numerous places about it, the figure was curved instead of square and like the voice most definitely belonged to a woman. Anne blinked the tears from her eyes and when her vision cleared as much as it was going to, could just about make out the woman's face in the light from the lamp she carried. It had at one time been very beautiful she could see, but it was now disfigured by scars and the nose was misaligned from multiple breaks that had never been set. Her skin was a milky white and still held onto some of the glow of youth and of someone who took care of themselves.

"Here." the woman said offering Anne a bowl of what looked like watery soup.

" It's not much, but it will help you get your strength back".

She inspected Anne's face and winced with sympathy.

"Once the swellings gone down, we'll get you something a bit more substantial".

Anne sipped gingerly from the bowl, gripping it in both hands so not to spill its contents. She discovered that the soup held a meaty flavor despite its thinness, and that her lips were a mess of splits.

11

Each sip bought pain and delicious warmth in equal measure. After she had eaten as much of the soup as she could manage, she looked to her benefactor and with only slight trepidation asked a torrent of questions all at once.

"Pardon my rudeness miss and not meaning to be disrespectful or to sound ungrateful but who are you, where am I an' 'ow did I get 'ere?"

The woman sighed and looked at Anne, as if judging her measure, and with her hand-held palm out, clearly indicating she wished not to be interrupted gave her answer.

"Your questions and no doubt many more will be answered in the morning. For now, sleep and regain your strength".

With that, the woman rose from Anne's bedside and turned to leave. Not content with having been told to wait Anne blurted out a demand.

"At least let me know your name if nothing else!"

The woman stopped and without turning replied,

"Mary. My name is Mary, and I will answer your questions and tell you my story on the morrow."

With that she left.

# Chapter three.

Pirate: a person who robs or commits illegal violence at sea or on the shores of the sea.

The morning light filtered through shuttered windows and along with the reduced swelling of her face confirmed that Anne was indeed onboard a ship. What surprised her was where aboard the ship she was. The room was sizable and opulent, that along with the cot she lay in told her that she was in the Captain's cabin.

"Good morning".

The sudden noise of the greeting startled Anne and she whipped her head up and around trying to find its source. The move caused her some nausea and more than a little pain, but Anne was relieved to discover that the only occupant in the room, other than herself, was Mary. She relaxed and then thought better of it, after all what did she really know about this woman. True she had thus far shown Anne only kindness and compassion, her wounds were treated, and her belly filled, but trust in the woman would need to be gained before she let her defence's down even a little. The aches and pains in her body were testament to the last time she had blindly trusted someone.

Mary leaned against a table that stood dominant in the centre of the room. She wore simple clothes, breeches made from a hard-wearing material and a cotton shirt that offered plenty of movement. Anne realised that the woman was dressed for work and judging from the state of the woman's hands which were covered in dirt and cuts fresh with blood, she wasn't scared to get stuck into any task. Realising that she was staring Anne sat herself up and once she had gotten comfortable returned the others greeting.

"Good morning," she said. "I take it it's you I have to thank for my being able to see another sunrise?"

Mary came over from the table and sat in the simple wooden chair beside the cot. A fleeting smile passed over her lips which was supposed to be reassuring, but Anne realised that the expression was one that Mary wasn't used too.

Clearing her throat before she spoke, Mary then looked Anne in the eye and in a slightly hoarse voice began to speak.

"I believe I promised you my tale."

She sighed deeply and Anne got the feeling that if Mary told her tale a hundred times it would be just as painful as the first.

"I was once like you, a pretty young thing who dreamed of being swept off her feet by a ship's Captain."

Anne wanted to object to the woman's assumption, but Mary held up her hand indicating that she needed Anne to keep quiet till her tale was complete.

"I too used to work in a tavern waiting tables. One night a new crew comes in and their Captain starts throwing his money about, boasting that they've just taken in a massive haul. They sat at one of my tables, so I served them their drinks and the Captain tips me well. This goes on for the next two nights. The crew comes in, boasting and recruiting. The Captain, turns out his name was Ned Low, always tips me handsomely and I have to admit to having had my head turned. On the fourth night Ned comes over and tells me that they're setting sail on the morning tide. He says how he's always liked me and how he'd like to show me his ship and give me a night to remember."

Mary paused at that point, the painful memories of about to happen to her etched upon her once pretty face. She took a tankard from the bedside table that had been intended for Anne and drank deeply. The simple act was enough to settle her nerves and she continued with her tale.

"The Captain walked me down to the harbour and I can't help but remember that it was such a beautiful night. The stars were out in full, and the sea breeze was cool and refreshing. The ship when it came into view appeared huge to me with three masts, and my heart raced as we climbed the gang plank.

15

I remember that all I could think at the time was if I played this right, I could be his girl. As soon as we were aboard and in the privacy of his cabin though, his whole demeanor changed. The gallant Captain had all been an act and once we were alone his true personality came out. He threw me to the floor and when I looked up into his face, confused at what had just happened, I met the real Ned Low. His features seemed to change before my eyes, growing darker and shadowed even though his cabin was well lit. He reached down and grabbed me by the hair and then dragged me to the middle of the room where a length of rope hung from one of beams. I cried out screaming for help and he laughed in my face, his breath suddenly fetid and hot where it had seemed sweet only moments before. "Scream all you like my dear", he taunted. "No one can hear you and even if they did, they wouldn't care". He bound my wrists together with the rope, before hauling me up so my feet barely touched the floor. His oily hands were then all over me like a writhing squid. I kicked at him but again he laughed and then slapped me so hard I nearly blacked out. Again he grabbed me by the hair, this time raising my face so that I was forced to see his. My chin grew wet with blood from where his blow had split my lips. Grinning at the sight he lent in and started to lick at the blood and then started to suck it from my lips like some kind of perverse kiss. For three days I hung from that beam while he did to me whatever deprived notion crossed his mind. On the fourth day I started to scream. I couldn't stop myself, I just kept screaming and screaming. I thought I was alone, Ned had left the cabin and thinking that it was to be my only chance to escape I pulled at my bonds.
But they were expertly tied, and each tug only tightened them more, so I snapped and that's when the screaming started."
Mary looked on the verge of hysteria, panting and sweating

16

as she spoke and had to take a moment to recompose herself and get her breathing back under control. Once she felt that she had calmed down she resumed her horrific tale. "I don't know how long I was like that, but I do know that I only stopped when the Captain burst into the room howling with laughter! "Scream! Scream all you like missy" he taunted. "It's just you and me, no one to interrupt us". Turns out the crew had all been dismissed on shore leave earlier that day so that Ned could have me all to himself. He took great pleasure, after cutting me down, in dragging me around the whole ship just to prove how alone we were. To prove he announced in the same way a civil man announces that he is going for a stroll that he was going to defile me on the upper deck. "It'll be romantic!" he chuckled. He dragged me out into the cool night air I could see that we were anchored out in the harbour of a busy port although I hadn't realised we had even sailed. Hoping to draw the attention of somebody on the shore I started screaming again, but every time I did, so did he, before laughing hysterically. Lying on the deck I remember thinking that it was such clear night, nothing but stars, far too beautiful a setting for what was about to happen. When he started to open my legs I tried to fight him off, something I hadn't been able to do before when I was roped up to the deck head. My resistance, small as it was, angered him. "What! Am I not good enough for you now?" he bellowed. "You think you're too pretty for a humble pirate Captain?" and with that he punched me in the face, breaking my nose in the process. "There, problem solved!" he said. Then he dropped to his knees and returned to his previous intentions, but when he pulled down his breaches, the drinking he had been doing that day had had an effect on his manhood. "This is your fault," he growled. "If you hadn't forced me to make you so ugly, I'd be able to get it up!" As payment for my digression, he backhanded me, breaking my cheek. "Now look at you, your even uglier," he said, sounding disgusted as he spoke. "Sorry" he continued "it's no good, I think we're gonna have to split up." With that he stood and dragged me by the ankle towards the edge of the ship. My hands tore at the wood beneath me ripping finger nails out as I tried to stop what was obviously about to be me death. My prayers were answered when the Captain stopped dragging me and bent down to pick me up so he could throw me overboard. With my hands still bound I grabbed at anything I could and found what looked like a little club. As his head came in, I swung with all my strength and hit him square on the temple. He stood blinking hard with a look of complete confusion on his wretched face before pitching over the side. It was daylight by the time I had enough strength to pick myself up off the deck. Taking in my surroundings I found that the ship was one of two in the harbour that morning. The ships boats were nowhere to be seen so were probably ashore with the crew. I knew that they would probably return at any moment, so the time was now to make my escape. I had no knowledge of sailing or how to operate a ship at the time but felt that if I cut the anchor line that I would drift with the morning tide. So that's what I did. I found an axe and although it took all I had, I managed to cut away the anchor and drift out to sea. That is how I came to be in possession of this fine ship."

At that Mary paused and spread her arms wide to indicate the ship that she was obviously very proud of.

"It took weeks before I finally ran aground. In that time I got my strength and health back, if not my good looks. The ship was well provisioned and so I wanted for nothing. So well provisioned in fact was the hold, with looted spices and silks, that when the people of the small Jamaican island I ran aground on came to investigate, I was able to pay them for repairs the ship needed, and for a crew to get me back to civilisation. I span them a yarn that I was the only survivor of a pirate raid to explain my predicament, and my face gave proof enough for that to be truth. When we set sail, it was into calm seas, and I was able to learn some basic seamanship on the way to Port Royal. When we docked with the other merchant ships, I bid my crew fair well and paid them a healthy sum for their help and silence. I had plans for this ship, plans I'd come up with during the voyage.

# Chapter four.

Revenge: something done to get even with
somebody else who has caused harm.

Over the next few weeks as her strength returned to her Anne learned more about what was in store for the ship which Mary had renamed "The Jenny's Revenge". She was also given the option, as all the other women aboard had been, to become a member of the ship's company. Anne felt she had no option but to accept the offer, after all, she owed this woman her life. She started her training the very same day hoping that she could help to make Mary's plan a reality. Mary's plan and the ship's rename were all based around one and the same thing, revenge. The crew, most of which Anne had now met, all had similar tales of woe as her own. Some were the widows of sailors killed by pirates when their ships had been taken. Some were the former lovers or wives of men who had turned to piracy and the left them scorned, destitute and beaten. Others like herself and Mary had been barmaids and prostitutes, treated like dirt, raped, beaten, and left for dead. Whatever their story all of these "Jenny's", a term often used by pirates when referring to women, all wanted the same thing, revenge. Mary had paid hard coin, traded or bartered with anything she could find within the ship's hold in order to get people to train her crew in the skills required to run a ship day to day on the high seas. She'd also found somebody willing to train one of her crew in hand-to-hand combat and the art of using a sword. For this task Mary had chosen Isabel, one of the first to join her crew, to become her Master at Arms. Once Isabel had learned all she could she had started a training program for the rest of the ship's company, a training program which Anne fully intended to start as soon as she had the strength. For the moment Anne had to start, as all new members to the crew had, by learning basic seamanship. She discovered she had a knack for knot tying but still lacked the strength to haul the rigging, although she had learned the theory. On her third week aboard, Anne joined the galley team where her former life as a bar wench was extremely useful. She waited the tables and served food whilst getting to know the crew. Mary had done well in her recruitment and the women of the ship's company had bonded in their goal, and Mary's vision of becoming pirate hunters. That was Mary's true intention for the "Jenny's revenge", to hunt and kill all of those and their kind responsible for what had happened to each and every member of her crew.

# Chapter five.

*Informant: somebody who supplies information or somebody who gives information to somebody else.*

*In* order to carry out her plans Mary needed informants. People who could gather the information she needed, such as the whereabouts or the name of the ship that their targets crewed, without being noticed. The best people she could think of for the job were the girls who worked in the bars and whore houses in every port. In most cases these women gave up their information willingly, as for every Tom that paid for their services, their were plenty who didn't. Mary would approach each of these women and bring her into the fold, one of the crew but land based. All they had to do was listen for the most part. Pirates loved to brag so all that was required was to pay attention and if specific names were mentioned, the names given by those aboard the Jenny, the girls were instructed to ply their trade and get everything they could out of the mark. In these case's Mary rewarded well for the danger that the girls had put themselves into. But as with all dangerous work, from time to time one of the land-based crew would find they had to become part of the permanent ship's company. Not all of the information she needed came from Mary's network of land crew. For every wronged woman there were just as many legitimate merchant or freelance traders who had come afoul of a pirate boarding. Most of the survivors of these encounters would find their way to one bar or another whilst in search of work and were more than ready to tell their tale of misfortune. Mary could see in many of these men the same desire for revenge as her own and although unwilling to take them on as crew, she recognised an opportunity when she saw one. Always wary when approaching a sailor in a bar, lest they got the wrong idea, she would proposition them and although she dismissed many, she gladly employed those who were willing to take her seriously. Information always required payment, but Mary was willing to use everything she had in order to get what she wanted. In most cases the old adages nothing is for free, and everything has its price was true, but for two cases, and those had only cost a promise.

# Chapter six.

*Katar: A push dagger from the Indian subcontinent, distinctive for its H shaped handle.*

The day that Anne had waited so very patiently for had
finally arrived. Her body was fully healed, and all of her
seamanship lessons had given her a leaner and stronger
physique. As she stood in front of the ships Master at
Arms, ready to start her weapons training, Anne tried not to
flinch as she was given the once over. She knew that this
inspection was important and would give the go ahead as to
whether or not a member of the crew was to be given
weapons training. She desperately hoped that she would be
able to pass muster and wouldn't be sent back to the galley.
"You look strong enough", Isabel said, her French accent
soft but her voice harsh.
"I've watched you these past few weeks. You work hard
and listen to what you're told. I like that."
Her gaze locked onto Anne's intense and intimidating.
"Mark my words young lady. If you can't keep up with my
training, you will be out! No second chances."
Isabel smiled at Anne as if confirming that she was pleased
with her decision. The smile held warmth but showed no
teeth, Isabel never showed her teeth. Truth be told she had
very few to show. They had been taken from her by a
drunken pirate. He had stumbled whilst coming out of a bar
and dropped his drink and as he looked up from the spilled
contents the first thing he'd seen was poor Isabel. Fate had
not been kind to Isabel that day, she was simply on her way
home from work, before this life she had been a chamber
maid at the Governor of Port Royals mansion.
"That's your bloody fault that is!"
The pirate had said, grabbing Isabel by the hair as she tried
to get by. "You owe me a drink!"
As he dragged her towards the bar Isabel started to scream.
She had hoped that it would alert people to her peril, but all
it actually did was anger her assailant.
"Gods, what a bleedin' racket!" he said, turning to put his
face in hers before shouting "Shut. Up!"

He then let go of her hair but only so he could swing a viscous back hand to Isabel's jaw. As the pirate's hand connected several of Isabel's teeth came out and landed on the floor at about the same time as she did. Seeing that the pirate bent and retrieved them and giggled.

"Oh, look at them," he said to nobody in particular.

"Look at how shiny white they are."

With a wicked gleam in his eye looked down at Isabel.

"Give me the rest of them!"

With that he continuously hit her as hard as he could only stopping when he got bored and no more teeth would come out. Isabel had never been pretty, quite a plain looking woman if truth be told, but after her beating, nobody wanted to look at her. The Governor had sacked her for who wants a chamber maid that no one could bare the sight of. Without money she lost her lodgings and that's how Mary had found her, begging on the streets with a makeshift hood hiding her face. The woman who now took Anne for her first training lesson was no longer a victim. Although quite demur at 5'4", her body was muscular and hard. Long hours of sword training had given her the strength to rival any man in melee combat. Now though, she only ever opened her mouth to talk or eat and then only enough to get the words out or food in, so when she did smile everyone knew it was genuine. Isabel led Anne to the quarter deck and handed her a wooden training sword. Or at least that's what Anna presumed it was. The swords blade was short and wide and instead of being attached in the traditional way to a cross guard and hilt it had a square structure, open on one end with a handle that went across instead of in with the blade.

Anne looked at it quizzically, and then at Isabel.

"It's called a Katar", the Master at Arms said. "It's an Indian design."

The choice of sword was no accident. The man who had

31

taught Isabel went by the name Anup Rai, and like the Katar was from India. He had served aboard a merchant vessel transporting spices from southern Asia to the rest of the world when they had been attacked by pirates. A fierce and bloody battle had ensued which the pirates had won. After plundering all that they wanted, the Captain had his crew set the ship alight and cast it adrift with the survivors of the ship's crew trapped below decks. Few had survived, Isabel's sword master being one of them. He had been one of the two who had agreed to offer his services for a promise. If Mary ever found those responsible for bringing such dishonor to them, he wanted the Captain's head and heart. Mary had given her promise in exchange for the pirate Captains name when it was learned and Isabel's training.

"As it was explained to me," Isabel said, "the Katar is elegant and quick. Perfect for those with a smaller build." Picking up a nearby Cutlass, Isabel swung it a few times before continuing.

"The Cutlass is a cumbersome and clumsy weapon designed with brute strength in mind. I am, and probably will remain one of the few aboard the Jenny's Revenge who can wield one".

Isabel returned the Cutlass and then picked up two training Katars.

"The beauty of these blades is that even the weakest of the ship's crew can wield two at once if properly trained." With that she broke into a series of complex moves, the two training blades becoming a blur before Anne's eyes.

The Master at Arms completed her maneuvers.

"My master taught me well and I in turn shall teach you," she said and once again smiled her tight-lipped smile at Anne.

"But for the mean time I believe we should work with just the one blade".

Relieved by the news Anne let out a sigh of relief.

# Chapter seven.

First mate; captain's second-in-command: an officer on a merchant ship or any non-naval vessel.

𝓜onths had passed since the morning that Anne had woken upon The Jenny's Revenge. The whole of the ship's company had been trained in their primary and secondary duties and the time had come to set sail. Mary didn't plan on going on the hunt just yet though. She wanted to see how the crew behaved when under sail and out of sight of land. The crew, for the mass majority, had been together for some time now, and in fact Anne was new newest recruit. As Mary had briefed the crew, they were to set sail for just over the horizon where if a dispute arose the girls couldn't simply walk off onto dry land to cool off. Like every other ship's Captain before her, Mary knew that the success of any ships company lay in their bonding together, to become more than just a crew, they had to become comrades-in-arms or better yet, sisters. The course had been plotted by her navigator, a young English girl by the name of Rose who had been left an orphan when her parents were killed on the crossing to the Jamaica's. The girl had no place in a fight but had shown a natural aptitude for maps. This trip would test Rose's abilities and reliability, whilst assuring Mary that she had the right girl in the right place. She knew that there would be changes in position of various members of the ship's company, but for now she was pleased with her decisions. As the ship slipped its moorings nobody paid it any more attention than any other ship of its kind. Mary had given every member of the ship's company a simple uniform of the same hard-wearing breeches as she wore, an airy cotton shirt and a bandana to keep the sweat and hair from their eyes. Many sailors wore their hair long so that, along with the non-descript clothing, the woman to all intents and purposes looked the same as any other sailor on a free trade vessel. The uniform was also deliberate in its design. It would be considered extremely out of the ordinary for a ship to set sail with women on its crew, they were still believed by many sailors to be bad luck at sea. It

was also cheap, hard wearing, and easy to come by in most ports.

As this was their first official outing, Mary had elected herself to be in charge, distributing the orders rather than the first mate as was traditional. She turned to her helmsman, a young Jamaican girl called Amy who was around seventeen or eighteen, directing her to stay within the shipping lane and then turn onto a westward heading when clear to do so. Amy acknowledged the order with a muted "Aye".

The girl's name was not really Amy, it was the one she had chosen when she had joined the crew. She had had her tongue cut out by a pirate landing party when she had stumbled across them as they replenished their fresh water supplies. One of the pirates had grown angry with her inability to speak English and had reckoned with his ship mates that,

"If she can't talk proper like us; then their aint no point in her avin' a tongue!"

With that they had pinned poor Amy down, pulled out her tongue as far as they could before slicing it off with a knife. As she lay on the ground, balled up and mewling in pain, one of her assailants had decided that she sounded like a cat and as their ship didn't have one, they should keep her as a pet. It then became Amy's job to catch the rats and vermin aboard the pirate's ship. The day Mary had found her Amy had been tied to the gangway by the neck, stopping rodents from boarding whilst the ship was in port. She was extremely malnourished, as cats only get to eat what they catch, and was happy to follow Mary when her tether was cut. Mary had taught her English and when she had offered the girl a list of names, she had chosen Amy as it was easy to say even with her missing tongue.

The Jenny's Revenge slipped from the harbour under minimal sails, Amy guiding her like a seasoned helmsman rather than someone on their maiden voyage. The ship was a three masted, Spanish built galleon that had been modified by its previous owner for speed and maneuverability over how much cargo it could hold. That being said the holds were typical of a pirate vessel. The mid deck floor had been raised making her holds larger than a similar vessel of her kind, plunder being more important than being able to walk without a stoop when below decks. That had probably been a problem for the previous crew but with their shorter stature, the women of the Jenny had no such problem. The ship had also been outfitted with a larger rudder and was wider in the beam allowing her to turn in quickly making it perfect for piracy and, Mary hoped, exacting revenge on those that the ship had no doubt been built for. Once they were in open waters Mary gave the order to hoist all sails as she wanted to know exactly what her ship could do. With full sails set, the Jenny's Revenge was a truly magnificent sight. Each sail, pregnant with wind, pulled at its rigging and caused the masts to creak in song. The increase in speed caused the wake to spread out around them and create a spray. The saltiness of that spay stung Mary's eyes and left a taste that al sailors knew in her mouth. She felt truly exhilarated.

"How fairs she Ms. Jones?" Mary called out to her first mate.

Ms. Jones looked from her position on the main deck to where her Captain stood on the half deck, an enigmatic smile on her face and gave her report.

"She fairs well Ma'am. All rigging is deployed including the Lateen and the Sprit. Both Mains look a little tired and will need replacing in time but are holding well. She's a fine ship Ma'am," her tone proper, her English accent decidedly upper crust.

"That she is," replied Mary.

"That she is. Thank you Ms. Jones."

Unlike most of the women aboard who had given up their surname when they had joined the ships company, leaving behind their family ties, Ms. Jones had done the opposite. Her husband had been an officer in the Royal Navy and had been killed during a skirmish with pirates. When the news was delivered to Ms. Jones it had crushed her. She had used all of the money they had saved, and favors owed to her husband to travel to Port Royal so that she could attend the funeral only to discover that his body had been lost at sea. The stress of the whole situation had paid too much a toll on Ms. Jones's mental health, leaving her suicidal. The night Mary had found her, the widower had been hysterical and trying to hang herself on one of the city's gallows. And so Ms. Jones had been saved and enlisted to the Jenny. As it turned out, she had picked up a fair bit naval knowledge from her late husband and was given the job of First mate. The sun was starting to set, and Mary was extremely pleased with the crew's performance. Tomorrow she would give the gun crews a chance to show their worth but for now it was time to reduce sails for the manning of the night watch.

"Ms. Jones. Strike the mainsails and prepare for night rigging," Mary ordered.

"Aye Aye Ma'am!" Ms. Jones replied and started bellowing orders as her Captain headed below decks.

# Chapter eight.

*Spyglass: a telescope that is small enough to be held in the hand.*

Mary was in a jubilant mood as she walked the upper decks, inspecting her ship to see how it had faired after its first night at sea. The night watch had done well, and they were only a few degrees off of their set course.

"SAILS OFF THE PORT BOW!"

Mary scanned the horizon in the area indicated but could see nothing. She looked to the woman in the crow's nest that had made the call and who still pointed direction of the sails. Before Mary could ask for details the lookout started to relay information she desired.

"Just over the horizon Captain. They just went to full sail, so I think they spotted us."

"Any idea who they are?" Mary asked the look out.

With that the woman pulled out a spyglass and studied the ship for several minutes before reporting.

"They're not flying colours of any kind Captain."

Mary feared the worst at this news. Many pirates were known to sail with no indicators of nationality, loyal only to themselves and their code. She knew a few of the merchant ships in the area had started to employ the same tactic in an attempt to confuse ships in their area into believing that they were one of their own.

"Wake the ship! Get everyone to their stations!"

Mary shouted to the officer of the watch.

Pulling out her own spyglass Mary scanned the heading given by the look out and found that the ship had cleared the horizon now and continued with a course set to intercept them. Although still too distant to make out many details, she could see that the ship was smaller than her own, most likely a sloop of some kind. There were only two reasons that she could think of for why another ship would set a direct course for another like that, and as they had not signaled that they were in distress it had to be the other reason, piracy. Mary knew she had to come up with a plan and fast. There was no point in trying to set the sails and run as there was no way that they would be able to get up to speed before the other ship was upon them. Still, her musings had given her the sparks of a plan.

"Ms. Jones!"

Mary was pleased to see that her First mate was already on deck and heading in her direction. Before the woman could answer to the hail, she was receiving orders.

"Ms. Jones, go down to the hold and break out some of the dresses we keep there."

The First mate looked confused by the order, but Mary knew there was no time for an explanation.

"Pick six of the women with no facial injuries and get them dressed up."

Still looking none the wiser Ms. Jones simply nodded and set about obeying the order. Turning to the next woman on deck Mary found it to be Anne.

"Come here." she ordered and directed the woman towards the mainmast.

"I want you to take a crew and drop the lower mainsail down to the deck."

Then Mary made sweeping motions with her hands and continued.

"Unfurl it and pull it out over the deck. Try to make it look like we tried to raise it and failed."

"Aye Ma'am." Anne said and then grabbing the first two women she saw set about doing as she had been ordered. Drawing her spyglass once more, Mary checked the position of the sloop, the ship still flew no colours, and reckoned they had fifteen minutes at most before they were on top of them. The Master at Arms was next on her list and Mary found her on the Halfdeck, fully armed and ready for action.

"Excellent Isabel. It looks like we have the same idea about who's coming to visit us." the Captain said admiring the woman's attire.

"Get the rest of the crew not already assigned a detail armed and ready below decks. Then get the gun crews to charge the cannons but leave them stowed."

As the Master at Arms rushed off to carry out the order, Ms. Jones appeared and reported that six of the crew were dressed and in makeup.

"Thank you Ms. Jones. I have a plan."

She smiled at her First mate so as to reassure her.

"Gather the whole crew below decks and I'll explain."

"Aye Captain!" the First mate replied but Mary was already turning to the port rail and drawing her spyglass. She hoped they had enough time for her plan to work.

# Chapter nine.

*Sloop: a single-masted sailing boat, rigged fore-and-aft, with one headsail extending from the foremast to the bowsprit.*

When the sloop came alongside the Jenny's Revenge, larboard to, it was greeted by six women of apparent refinement, in a state of distress. Grappling hooks bit into the Jenny's rails and gang planks were quick to follow. Their boarding party consisted of eight men with Cutlasses in their belts and muskets tucked into bandoleers. None of them had weapons in hand, after all, why bother for a few helpless women.

"Ladies!" a flamboyantly dressed young man said. "I am Captain James Smith. Now, what seems to be the problem?"

Mary listened closely to the initial encounter below decks, ear pressed to the deck head and at the mention of the Captains name, looked to her crew. None of them had reacted in anyway at the man's greeting so Mary figured that he must either be new to the game or the Caribbean. On deck one of the newly formed decoy crew said in an exaggerated breathless voice,

"Oh Captain, thank goodness you are here!"

As she did, she swept the back of one hand across her brow in a pretense of distress.

"We were on our way to Port Royal when we were attacked by pirates!" Her voice was all a quiver when she said the word pirate.

Captain Smith eyed the women before him, then turned to his men.

"Did you hear that lads, they were attacked by pirates!"

"Oh my god Captain," replied one of his men, voice full of sarcasm. "It's lucky we 'appened on by!"

"That it is!" Smith replied with laughter.

"So ladies, what did you do during this 'pirate' attack?" he asked the women, over emphasising pirate as he did.

One of the other women continued the ruse, her voice quick, her bosom heaving as if excited just to be in the presence of these men.

"We hid in our cabin Sir while the men hid its door in turn behind cargo. We took all our valuables to, so as to protect them."

At the mention of valuables, the look of lust in the eyes of Smith and his men was joined with one of greed. Wrapping an arm around Lucy, Smith indicated towards a door which he hoped would lead them to the ship's interior.

"Why don't you show us this little hidey hole of yours ay ladies?"

His voice, although still cheery, had taken on a sinister edge.

Smith's boarding party then moved in on the rest of the decoy crew, herding them like cattle, the look in their eyes and their body language evidence enough to their intensions. Mary came down from where she had been listening at the deck head and as loudly as she dared, ordered those she had selected to be her ship's protectors and boarding party to hide and stand-by. She had dowsed as many of the lamps as she dared so that only the area in the middle of the deck was dimly illuminated. Captain Smith and his men entered the interior of the ship with their 'rescued' ladies in distress, and as soon as they were in the gloomy confines of the ship's interior, he and his men dropped all pretense about their intensions for the women. Although she had suspicions from the very moment that the sloop had cleared the horizon, Mary had been hoping to be proven wrong. She had hoped that these were just ordinary sailors coming to the aid of a ship in distress. One of the men unable to contain himself any longer, grabbed the women in front of him by the hair and started tearing at her dress. That single act confirmed Mary's beliefs that they were indeed pirates. Smith turned and laughed at his man's eagerness.

"Easy matey!" he guffawed. "Save some for the rest of the crew!"

At that he grabbed Lucy by the back of the neck and
squeezing hard said,
"Now missy, I believe you were going to show me your,
valuables."
This last word he dragged out, making it sound obscene and
as he did, he looked Lucy up and down, licking his lips as
he did so. Whilst all of this happened, Mary and the
boarding party slid from their hiding places in the darkened
corners and unsheathed their Katars.
"NOW!"
Mary bellowed and she and her crew sprang into action.
Isabel flew from her hiding place, a Katar in each hand. She
embedded the one in her left hand almost to the hilt in the
back of one man and the throat of another with her right as
he fumbled for his cutlass. Mary had decided to take out
Smith personally and took great pleasure in staring the man
in his eyes as she punched her blade strait into the man's
heart. The rest of the crew took out the remaining pirates in
quick succession which allowed Mary to go up to the gun
deck. She'd had the gun crews move their cannons into
position, but not so far as to open the gun ports. Now as she
came up on to the same deck she screamed,
"All guns, Fire!"
At her order all the cannons on the larboard side were run
out into firing position, their ports open and in unison all
six cannons fired. At such short range the damage was
devastating. Having dealt with Smith's men in the hold, the
Jenny's boarding party now raced out onto the upper deck
where they were greeted by the sight of what remained of
the sloop sinking beneath the waves.
The Master at Arms as head of the boarding party was the
first on deck. She moved to the rails and surveyed the
wreckage with satisfaction, but as she did so spotted
survivors in the water.
"Muskets to the Larboard rail!" She ordered.

"Leave no survivors."

# Chapter ten.

*Decoy: somebody or something used to deceive or divert attention, especially in order to lure somebody into a trap.*

The moral aboard the Jenny's Revenge was high that night. Mary had been impressed by the crew's performance that day. If she was honest with herself, she had been seriously concerned that the women wouldn't be able to perform when the moment arose, and she included herself in those worries. Training was all good and well but in reality, you could never truly tell how anybody would react in the heat of a real situation until they were thrust into it. A few of the women had stood out and made a real impression upon Mary during the exchange with Smith and his men. Isabel of course came at the top of the list. The woman's strength and courage were more than most men could ever hope to muster but her recklessness was something that Mary felt she may need to keep an eye on. Attacking two men at once on their first skirmish could be considered as fool hardy.

Anne had also impressed her. Mary had to admit that when the woman had first joined the ship's company, after recovering from her injuries, she thought that Anne would be little more than a Galley hand, or at best an able seaman. Surprisingly the woman had shown a more than capable ability with the Katar and had kept her head during the battle. Mary decided that if Anne continued to perform as she had today, and when the situation arose, that she would promote her to a more prominent position within the crew. She felt that Lucy, one of the decoy party, had also done herself proud, keeping her composer whilst leading the men to their death. She decided to make her the head of the decoy party there and then. The girl had very little in the way of face-to-face experience with Pirates and was part of the crew because she had been made homeless when it had been set ablaze during a raid on their settlement by Captain Morgan. Morgan had set his sights on the Spanish Main in order to make his wealth. Most of Lucy's village had fled at the sight of Morgan's fleet but Lucy's son was ill, so they had been unable to. Lucy had rescued the boy from the flames, but smoke and the boy's condition had seen him perish before the night was through. It was well known to all that Morgan operated out of the Jamaica's and so Lucy had stowed away on the next vessel she could find in hopes of one day being able to confront her son's killer. She had made it to Port Royal, but the journey had taken a terrible toll on her health. Mary had found her almost blind with dehydration roaming the docks begging for help. It was time for the evening meal and Mary was eager to spend it with her crew. It boosted the women's moral to see their Captain amongst them, showing that she didn't consider herself above anybody else on the ship. Mary wanted to discuss the day's events with the other members of the ship's company and get a feel for what they thought of her on the spot decision making, and the plan she had come up with. Mary felt that it had gone well and wanted to use it again, but with a few tweaks. Walking into the ship's main area, the Captain of the Jenny's Revenge was greeted by the sight of the evening meal already being served to all those not on duty. As she walked among the women already bonded as a ship's company, she now observed that they were bonding in their specialised units. She made a point to stop and talk with the various groups, commending them on the day's action. The Gunnery crews she praised on their swiftness at being able to prime the cannons and have no miss fires. From there she went to the women who had served as bait. For many of these women, like Lucy, it had been their first true encounter with pirates as much of the decoy party was made up of widowers. Mary was concerned that this group of women more than any other may be suffering from the trauma of coming face to face with those who had destroyed their lives.

This was not the case though. If anything, the Decoy party seemed the most jubilant of the entire crew. After thanking the Cook for her meal Mary scanned the crowd for Isabel. The woman sat with her back to her Captain, but her muscular form made her easy to spot amongst the crew. Making her way over to her Master at Arms Mary noted two things, the woman sat with the boarding party, and they all sat in complete silence. Coming up to their table, Mary cleared her throat so as to gain attention and invited her Master-at-Arms to come dine with her. Once sat at their own table she asked,

"Are the women alright?"

Indicating with a nod of her head the members of the boarding party.

"They're coming to terms with themselves Captain," Isabel replied. "They've all trained for it but none of us has killed before today and these girls did it face to face."

"I understand."

Mary said her tone understanding. Smith hadn't been the first man she had killed, but she knew that taking a life needed time for recovery.

" Keep an eye on them. If any of them looks like they'll hesitate next time, change them. No judgment on their character."

Ms. Jones came to the table and after asking permission to join them sat next to Isabel.

"Ladies," Mary addressed the two women. "We need to discuss today's events."

# Chapter eleven.

*Master-at-Arms: a non-commissioned officer aboard a naval vessel who is responsible for maintaining order and enforcing discipline in the ship's company.*

The three women discussed the day's events at length. All aspects of the Jenny's Revenge's first days at sea were reviewed. How the crew had handled the ship's day to day duties, raising the sails, moving around in the rigging and sea sickness. Before long the discussion inevitably came around to their encounter with Captain Smith and his crew. All three of them were in agreement that although Mary's plan had worked, it was in need of improvement. Mary believed that the plan would only remain useful if they continued to leave no survivors. She surmised that if they left even one person alive, then sooner or later word would get out about a ship full of women tempting crews in before attacking and killing all hands. Sure, it may not be believed at first, but once the word was out then their plan would be useless.

"Isabel, how are the boarding party?"

Mary asked her Master-at-Arms. The woman knew what her Captain was really asking was could the women under her command kill, without question, every member of every crew they encountered.

"At the moment Captain I believe that they can do what you're asking of them. I don't believe that there's a woman aboard who would disagree with that aspect of the plan." The woman's frankness in her statement put Mary's mind at ease. She knew it was a lot to ask of the crew, but no Pirate had ever shown any mercy to the members to them or their family and she didn't intend to show any mercy in return. It was Ms. Jones's turn to raise her anxieties over the Captains plan.

"If I may ma'am, I have some concerns over the safety of the women, decoy and boarding party alike." the First mate said.

"How so?" questioned Mary.

"Firstly with the decoy party."

Ms. Jones indicated with a nod to the group who still wore

their dresses.

"They have no protection until they are below decks. Until then they are on their own with nothing but pretty garments."

"What can we do," Isabel interrupted. "If we arm them or leave someone on deck with them then the trap would be ruined."

"I don't know," confessed Ms. Jones." But they need something."

A polite cough drew the attention of the three women and as one they looked up to see Anne stood at the head of the table.

"Yes Anne, can we help you?"

Mary asked with mild irritation at being interrupted.

"Sorry ma'am, I didn't mean to over 'ear, but I was clearing the tables and, well, I do have a suggestion." the young girl blurted out.

Mary prompted Anne to go on, her irritation replaced with intrigue.

"When I worked in the Cabin boy, I noticed that a lot of sailors wore a wide leather belt. I once asked one of em why and he told me it was for his back while working the decks, savvy?"

Again Isabel interrupted.

"I fail to see how this helps in our situation!"

Her French accent thickening with her irritation.

"Please bear with."

Anne said to the Master-at-Arms and then continued.

"I used to wear a bodice for similar reasons. It's hell on the back serving drinks and men!"

She went to laugh at her own joke but received severe scowls from the other women so continued.

"I was thinking, if we combined the two making a bodice out of thick leather, it could protect from swords and knives and would blend in with the girl's dresses."

The three women at the table considered this and after a short while it was Isabel who piped up her appraisal of Anne's idea.

"I like it!" the Master-at-Arms said. "We could expand the idea for the boarding party by having leather doublets which would give protection to the shoulders as well."

Mary nodded her approval of the idea.

"As soon as we make port, I'll release the funds. We'll have bodices for the decoy party and doublets for the boarding."

Decision made she turned to her First mate.

"Ms. Jones you mentioned some concerns. I believe we've covered the first, what's next?

"I don't like that when the decoy party brings the Pirates down into the ship that we have to get in so close and take them on with the Katars."

"What would you suggest?" Isabel asked the First mate.

"We need to maintain the element of surprise and for that we need silence. So muskets are out which leaves us only with the blade."

Once more Anne coughed for attention, this time though nobody interrupted her.

"When I was a little girl my Dad was a sailor, which is 'ow we came to be 'ere, and he used to tell me stories of old English sailing ships like the Mary Rose. Well before they had muskets the Navy used crossbows. Couldn't we use them too?"

"Crossbows?" Mary raised a questioning eyebrow at Isabel.

"It could work Captain." the Master-at-Arms said. "They would solve the problem of having to get up close and they're almost silent."

"Where would we get crossbows?" Mary questioned them all.

"Ma'am," Ms. Jones answered her Captain.

"There isn't much you can't get in Port Royal. Ironically the people we need to see in order to get what we want are the very people we want to use them on."

She gave a shrug, and a wry smile crossed her lips.

"Pirates."

# Chapter twelve.

*Quartermaster: Responsible for keeping the peace and settling disputes on a ship. Senior member of the gangway staff responsible for ships security.*

The problem with Port Royal was it was full of pirates. They walked down every street and drank in every pub, tavern and whore's parlor. It was for this reason that instead of docking at one of the various wharfs available, Mary had the Jenny's Revenge anchored out in the bay and used boats to get ashore. This solved two problems. Firstly, that even dressed in their working clothes, under close scrutiny somebody might work out that the ship was crewed entirely by women, drawing unwanted attention and questions that would be too hard to simply explain away. Nobody paid any real attention to the coming and goings of the various row boats that constantly came and went so their use would help keep the identity of the crew a secret. Secondly, if something were to happen ashore, one way or another the ships company could return to the Jenny. Alongside the ship could be blockaded or boarded with ease. Those were the two things that Mary feared the most, that if and when the word got out about them, they wouldn't be safe and one or both of those two things could happen. For now, the Jenny's revenge looked like any of the many other merchant ships out in the harbour, except for one thing. As they held no cargo in their holds the Jenny sat high in the water compared to those around her. To help maintain their cover Mary had decided that they needed to start hauling goods. Most merchant ships ferried whatever they could around the Caribbean to the various settlements and a decent Captain could make good coin working just the local area, distributing whatever the bigger ships brought in from around the world. The taking on of cargo could kill two birds with one musket shot. It would provide the perfect cover story for why the Jenny was in and around the various ports and shipping lanes around the Caribbean and the money that they could make would provide vital funds, allowing Mary and her crew to continue with their crusade.

For the most part Mary had the crew come and go into Port Royal at night making it harder to identify the women. In a place like Port Royal, it wasn't uncommon for movements around the harbour in the dead of night, it was filled with pirates after all. That helped Mary as well, when tracking pirates, move when they do. The bars and brothels were always full at night which allowed the shore crew to gather information with less risk of being discovered. This particular evening Mary wanted to find a pirate for an entirely different reason to her normal exacting revenge on them, arms dealing. In particular, crossbows. Ms. Jones had been right, the best place to get weapons in any and every port in the Caribbean was from pirates. They didn't care who they sold to as long as they saw profit. Mary had chosen Isabel for the task at hand. She was to seek out her weapons trainer and get him to be an intermediary for them. Again, this would reduce the risk of suspicion. Even in a place like Port Royal, a woman trying to buy any kind of weapon in the numbers that they needed would pique the interest of many a pirate, merchant or lawman alike. Whereas using Mr Anup Rai, would not. It also allowed Isabel to reassure her teacher that they, or more to the point Mary, had not reneged upon her promise.

Ms. Jones in the meantime had gone to try and broker a deal to haul goods to help build upon the illusion that they were a simple merchant vessel. She was only to try for something small as none of them had any idea when it came to making trade deals or hauling goods. A few of the other women had been sent out to get provisions. They took simple everyday dresses with them in order to get changed once ashore. Mary reasoned that many of the traders of Port Royal would be inclined to be more honest when dealing with a member of the fairer sex. With so many members of the ship's company coming or going Mary knew that she needed someone to keep track of who was or wasn't on board. She believed that the position was known as "Quartermaster" and that whoever held the post was responsible for the security of the ship and its crew whenever they made port or were in harbour. The Quartermaster was also to carry out the duties of Helmsman. Mary already had a Helmsman in the form of Amy, although it never hurt to have another, but she decided that her Quartermaster would concentrate on ships security, working closely with the Master-at-Arms. As Captain it was she who had the last say on who held what position on her ship and she had already decided that it would be filled by Anne. The woman had demonstrated that she was a capable as a seaman during the sea trials as well as in times of crisis such as the skirmish with Smith and his pirate crew. Anne had also proven that she was intelligent and could think on her feet. It was after all she who had come up with the ideas for the use of leather armour and crossbows. Anne was without a doubt suited for the job. She found Anne in her usual haunt of working in the ship's galley. It seemed that you could take the working girl out of the tavern, but old habits died hard. As soon as she spotted her Captain, Anne beckoned the woman to an empty table and asked if there was anything she could get her.

"Come, sit with me," Mary said. "I have something I want to talk to you about."

Instantly Anne looked worried. Although she had been a member of the ships company for six months now, she still felt that she wasn't truly a part of the crew. Mary hoped that by giving the woman a proper position, Anne would finally feel that she belonged on the Jenny's Revenge.

"Please," Mary said gently but firmly and indicated to the seat opposite her. "Relax, you're not in trouble, quit the opposite in fact."

Anne did as asked and sat but instead of relaxing into the

seat she sat on its edge looking confused and worried.

"I'll get to the point."

Mary said quickly and continued so for the rest of what she had to say. "Anne, I want you to be the ship's Quartermaster. You'll be responsible for ensuring that all members of the crew are accounted for as well as the security of the ship whenever we are at anchor. As such you will be working closely with Isabel, but you will not be a member of the boarding party."

She paused long enough to catch her breath and take in the other woman's look of disbelief.

"So, what say you?"

True to character Anne's words come out in such a flurry that they threatened to trip over each other.

"Well if you think I'm up for the job, then yes says I! I'll be your Quartermaster!"

Mary smiled and looked at the woman sat before her with genuine affection.

"Anne I can honestly say that I can think of no better person for the job."

# Chapter thirteen.

*Tortuga: A Caribbean Island forming part of Haiti. A major centre and haven for pirates in the 17th century.*

*I*sabel was the first back on board and was greeted by Anne in her new role as Quartermaster.

"Where's the Captain?"

The Master-at-Arms blurted out.

"In 'er cabin. Why? What's so urgent?"

"Get some of the crew to help you with those."

Isabel ordered and pointed to the pile of crossbows which sat in the keel of the away boat.

"Then take them to the Captain's cabin. I have some important news to tell her."

As Isabel hurried off Anne shouted over to three members of the crew who were taking in some air on the upper deck. Having retrieved the crossbows and their ammunition, the four women followed Isabel's order and headed to the Captain's quarters. After placing the new arsenal onto the table in the middle of the room they turned to take their leave.

"Thank you ladies," Mary said. "Anne, if I could ask you to stay. I think you should hear what Isabel has to say."

Isabel raised an enquiring eyebrow at her Captain.

"Master-at-Arms, meet your new Quartermaster. The two of you will be working together in the interest of the ship's security. As such I believe that Anne should be present for your news."

Mary directed them to sit at the table.

"So, what is so important that you needed to charge into my quarters as soon as you got back?"

She asked, eyebrows raised, lips pressed tight in a mixture of concern and dread. She feared that whatever the news may be, it probably wasn't good.

"As per your orders Captain I sought out Anup Rai and as you can see," Isabel made a sweeping motion with her hands over the contents of the table.

"With his help we were able to acquire all that we wanted."

"Very impressive."

68

The Captain stated picking up one of the weapons to inspect it.

"Were they hard for him to obtain?"

"We got a few here and a few there so as not to raise suspicion." Isabel replied.

"It was when he bought the last couple that he discovered the news which I am about to tell you. News that involves a promise to be repaid."

At the mention of the promise the colour drained from Mary's face so that she looked ashen and sickly. There were two promises that she had made but the one to Anup Rai was the one she hoped deep down would never have to be cashed in. After a short uncomfortable silence Mary indicated for Isabel to continue.

"As you know, my teacher never knew the name of his assailant, but he could never forget what he and his crew looked like. You can imagine how he felt when walking into a tavern, he saw one of the men who had left him to die."

Anne knew exactly how Anup Rai felt, as like so many aboard the Jenny's Revenge, she had been left in the same predicament.

"Fearing that he might be recognized Anup Rai told me how he'd worked his way behind the man so as to listen to what he had to say. Unsurprisingly the man was boasting about how they were in for a good haul next trip. When asked who he sailed under he said, "None other than Captain L'olonnais, so expect to see a crimson tide upon our return!"

Anup Rai knew this must be the Captain he had nearly lost his life to, so listened for details of his whereabouts."

Concerned for her Captains wellbeing Anne closely watched over her for fear that she may pass out. The woman was truly gripped by fear at the revelation of Anup Rai's aggressor as they all should have been.

Francois L'olonnais was without a doubt one of the most ruthless buccaneers to sail on any ocean, let alone the one around the Jamaica's. It was rumored that after capturing some Spanish troops, he had used his cutlass to cut out and eat the heart of one of them in order to gain information and beheaded an entire ships company solely for being Spanish, save for one to tell the tale. The man had single-handedly declared war on the Spanish and was known as "The bane of Spain."

Mary rubbed her face with both hands feeling as she did her disfigured nose and scars. Permanent reminders of why they were doing this. The thought of going up against someone as callous as L'olonnais was indeed terrifying, but she hadn't gotten into the revenge business just to fall at the first hurdle.

"When and where are they settin' sail?"

Anne asked. She like everybody else in the Caribbean had heard of the stories but tried not to let it show how much they scarred her.

"Anup Rai discovered that as the man became more intoxicated his tongue became a waterfall of information. He ordered a bottle of rum and when it came instructed the barmaid to place it on the man's table and walk away. The bottle was barely half gone before what he was seeking came forth."

Anne and Mary both subconsciously leaned in towards Isabel. Trepidation and fear painted their faces in equal measure at what the Master-at-Arms was about to reveal.

"They set sail on the morning tide headed for Tortuga. From there they intend to hit the trade routes between Nassau and here."

Mary slumped back into her chair, her mind in a whirl.

"Then we have 'bout a week before it's likely that we shall see L'olonnais."

Anne thought out loud.

"Maybe longer, 'pending on the wind."

"Quartermaster. Is my First mate aboard?"

Anne bolted upright in her chair and tried to match the tone her Captain had just used.

"Not yet Ma'am. She's still ashore attempting to secure us a cargo."

Mary nodded an acknowledgment then stood and stepped away from the table so that she could see both women equally.

"The strategy we used against Smith and his men will not work against a pirate like L'olonnais."

Trying to throw of her feelings of trepidation she said in as official a voice as she could muster.

"As soon as the First mate is back onboard, we shall meet in my quarters to draw a plan for battle, for that ladies is what I fear we are about to have."

# Chapter fourteen.

*Musket: a shoulder gun with a long barrel and a smooth bore, used between the 16th and 18th centuries.*

With Ms. Jones back onboard, having secured a modest yet profitable cargo of salted pork to be delivered to Nassau, the senior officers of the crew of the Jenny's Revenge gathered around the table in the Captain's quarters.

"Ladies, thank you for coming."

Mary said her tone of voice flat and official to indicate the severity of their meeting.

"For the sake of Ms. Jones, we are about to face one of the fiercest pirates to ever sail these or any other waters. This is not the encounter I would have chosen for our first official outing but we…"

She paused and reconsidered her words.

"I made a promise to Mr. Anup Rai. He held up his side of the bargain so now I need to uphold mine."

"Who are we to face?"

Ms. Jones asked. She was well aware of the promise her Captain had made to Anup Rai and knew full well that the woman would rather die than break her word. Mary looked Ms. Jones strait in the eye and slowly and clearly, so there could be no mistake, told her their adversary's name.

"L'olonnaise!"

Ms. Jones repeated, her voice high and reedy evidently shocked by the revelation.

"The man is ruthless, and his crew follows suit! How exactly are you proposing that we go up against someone like that?"

"What I propose,"

Mary said her tone calm so as to reassure the other women in the room and to hide her own terror at the situation.

"Is that we use similar tactics to those that we used against Captain Smith and his crew but with a number of changes."

Mary turned and addressed her Master-at-Arms.

"Isabel, you did a wonderful job of securing us the crossbows. I've had a chance to inspect them, and I believe

74

that they will work perfectly with our original plan. That being said, I do not want L'olonnaise or any member of his crew to set one foot aboard this ship!"

Although her voice was shrill come the end of her statement, there was no mistaking the iron in her words. Returning her attention to encompass all of the women in her council, Mary asked a single worded question, "Suggestions?"

The other three women in the room looked at each other clearly unprepared for the question but, once again, it was Anne who came forward with a solution.

"Ma'am, perhaps we could use Blunderbusses?"

"What is a Blunderbuss?" Isabel asked.

"Well,"

Anne started and the other women knew that the explanation was coming by way of a story.

"Quite a few different navy's use 'em including the British an' the Dutch. They're sort of like a cross between a musket and a pistol but with a bloody great barrel that can fire just about anything that will fit in it apparently. I used to have a Tom who had one. Always going on about how powerful it was. Used to pay me to do things with......."

"Thank you Anne."

Mary interrupted the girl before she could take her tale any further.

"And how do you propose we use these Blunderbusses?"

"Well, I was thinking we could add a few more girls to the decoy party and then they could 'ave 'em hidden away. Then when L'olonnais comes along side they whip em out and boom!"

"Fantastique!"

Isabel cheered with a clap of her hands and Mary nodded in agreement.

"Yet again Anne, your former life has given you the knowledge to provide us with a solution."

Ms. Jones praised the girl before turning to her Captain.

"I also have a proposal. Chain shot for the cannons."

When everyone returned a look of incomprehension, just as they all had for the Blunderbuss, Ms. Jones knew that she too would have to offer up an explanation.

"My late husband told me about them. It's essentially two cannon balls linked together with chain, which when fired causes them to flail through the air destroying anything they come into contact with."

"An excellent suggestion Ms. Jones,"

Mary told the First mate though her tone was tinged with doubt.

"One question though, would we be able to lay our hands on some?"

"I believe so."

Ms. Jones replied.

"There are some members of the Royal Navy who served with my husband who may be sympathetic to our cause. Especially those who were with him when he died."

Her voice held its usual no nonsense tone but all present could see the tension in the woman's neck and shoulders as she talked about the lost love of her life. Quickly moving on so as to spare her friend any further anguish Mary cocked a questioning eyebrow at Anne.

"Body armour?"

"Yes Captain. It will be ready before we set sail."

The Quartermaster reported.

" A few of the girls have been busy so the corsets and doublets have now been made. They're now being boiled in brine to harden them."

She paused and scratched her head in thought.

"Don't suppose we can get something to hold a Blunderbuss so it can be worked into the corsets?"

"First we need to get some." Isabel told her.

"Once again that will be up to you Isabel."

Mary told the Master-at-Arms.

"Go to Anup Rai and assure him that my promise to him will soon be fulfilled. Then impress upon him the urgency of our need and ask him once more to become our intermediary."

"Aye Captain. I'll leave at first light with some the crew and make it so."

"I to will leave at first light and travel to Fort Charles where some of my husband's former colleagues are based." Ms. Jones stated.

"Excellent."

Mary said rising from her chair.

"Let our Quartermaster know who you are taking with you and God speed ladies."

# Chapter fifteen.

Half deck: the command deck and the site for most navigation.

$\mathcal{B}$ack out on the open seas, all sails set for their
encounter with L'Olonnais, Mary stood on the half deck
and watched as Isabel drilled the decoy party on using their
newly acquired Blunderbusses. It had looked as though
their plan had been scuppered before it had even started,
when Isabel had returned empty handed, but Ms. Jones's
morning had gone extremely well. She had managed to
meet with one of the survivors of the encounter in which
her husband had been killed. As luck would have it, he was
now the stores master of the northern garrison of Port
Royal, Fort James. Ms. Jones had confided in the man and
found that he was willing to do anything in order to get
revenge on the piratical scum for what they had done to
him and his crew mates. Come the end of the meeting Ms.
Jones had secured eight Blunderbuss and twenty 5lb chain
shot for their cannons. The structure of their original plan
hadn't been changed that much from the chance meeting
with Captain Smith. The main difference was that there
would be no luring of the boarding party and no trap sprung
in the ship's hold. The intension this time was still to lure
the boarders to come over but to only let them make it part
way before the decoy party let them have it with their
Blunderbusses. Two things were to then happen at the
sound of gunfire. The Jenny's own boarding party were to
emerge from below decks to take out any survivors or
anyone else on the upper deck with musket and pistols. At
the same time the gun crews were to haul the cannons into
position and open fire. Half of the guns would be loaded
with standard cannonballs and aimed at the water line. The
other, loaded with chain shot, were to be aimed high so as
to hopefully take out the upper decks and masts. Mary felt
this new strategy would cause so much damage and
confusion that her crew wouldn't have to enter into
hand-to-hand combat. A cry of frustration snapped Mary
out of her reverie. One of the decoy party had missed her

Blunderbuss, a mistake that would cost them dearly in the real battle. Mary looked down in time to see Isabel giving the woman in question a dressing down.

"What seems to be the problem Master-at-Arms?"

"It's the latest version of the drill Ma'am!"

Came an exasperated reply.

"The women keep missing their weapons!"

Since obtaining them, the decoy party had tried numerous ways to hide and then fire the bulky weapons. Their first idea had been to simply put them on the deck but as the ship had moved, so to had the Blunderbusses, making it almost impossible to reach down, grab them and come up to a firing position quickly. Next, they had decided to hide them with in the folds of their dresses. This plan also had its complications. More often than not the oversized guns would get caught up in the fabric of the dress, stopping its owner from coming up to aim. One of the women had then suggested that they should somehow mount the weapons to their backs and then stand in two rows. The front row could then simply bend over whilst the back grabbed the weapon and fired. Everyone including Isabel and Mary had agreed that this plan was their best shot at success. Extra strapping and blocks were made to hold the Blunderbusses in place on the corsets that the decoy party now wore. Again though there were problems with the plan. It was hard for the women in the back row to step in and grab the weapons to fire. They either couldn't get their fingers to the trigger or missed altogether. Anne had now joined the women on the upper deck and after watching the decoy party struggle with the drill for a short while asked if she could offer a recommendation.

"This idea is a good'un." She said to Isabel.

"You're just goin' about it all wrong."

"Please."

The Master-at-Arms replied, drawing the word out and

coating it with more than a hint of sarcasm.

"Do enlighten us."

Anne stepped to the nearest woman with a gun strapped to her back.

"The two rows are spaced to far apart for starters."

She then placed herself right behind the woman in such a way that it looked as though she were caressing her back.

"You should be tryin' to look all vulnerable, but alluring at the same time so as to draw your targets in."

Without warning the Quartermaster screamed "BEND!" and the woman in front of her did as ordered allowing the rest of the party to see that Anne's hand was already in position on the Blunderbuss.

"BOOM!"

She shouted with glee.

Isabel looked at Anne in complete surprise before barking new orders.

"Right ladies! The Quartermaster has kindly shown us how it's done. So let's get to it shall we!"

# Chapter sixteen.

Nassau: Town on the island of New Providence in the Bahamas. Would become known as the Republic of Pirates between 1706 and 1718. It's here that the pirate "code of conduct" was established.

For three days the Jenny's Revenge had traversed the trade routes between Nassau and Port Royal under minimal sails. They had already been into Nassau to deliver their cargo and had taken on another. Whilst there Mary had sent members of the decoy party out in their dresses to gain information and spread the word that a Spanish galleon had been seen taking a fine cargo into its holds. It was well known that L'Olonnais had a deep hatred of the Spanish, and it was Mary's hope that by baiting the trap, word would get back to him. At that present moment the Jenny and her crew were starting to believe that they would have to deliver their present cargo and find another before heading back out. Provisions were also starting to get low, and Ms. Jones had begun drawing up a rationing plan that would allow them to stay out for two more days. Mary had made the decision that if their target didn't appear by sunset the following day then she would place them on a heading straight into Port Royal. A flicker of wind filled the sails and blew a stray lock of Mary's hair into her face causing a momentary distraction. As she scolded herself for being unkempt the lookout hollered.

"Sails off the starboard aft quarter!"

Mary span on the spot, drawing her spyglass as she did so. From her position on the half deck, she could see that the ship behind them was on a bearing to intercept with full sails allowing them to gain fast upon them.

"They're flying the red!"

Reported the lookout able to see more from her vantage point. The "red" she referred to, was the flag under which most pirates sailed, though in recent times, many in the Caribbean had started to use a black flag with a skull upon it, commonly referred to as the "Jolly Rodger". Many still flew the red, and Mary knew that L'Olonnais was among them, as its meaning of spare no one, struck fear into the hearts of many seafarers.

"HANDS TO ACTION!" she roared. "HANDS TO ACTION!"

At once all members of the crew moved to their assigned duties. The deck crew grabbed at the main sail and arraigned it so as to give the image of an intended but failed use. The decoy party disappeared below decks to get changed and Mary knew that the boarding party would be helping them to dress and prime their Blunderbusses before preparing their own weapons. The gun crew already had the cannons primed and loaded, it took too long to prepare them so they had been sailing with them charged and ready, but although their weapons were prepared, Mary knew that the crew would be lighting the slow burning matches and checking each cannons rigging. Those members of the crew without assignment were to draw Katars from the armoury just in case they took on boarders and their own boarding party became overwhelmed. These women were to wait in the cargo hold, out of the way, until needed. As the ship closed the distance, Mary used her spyglass to closer inspect their adversary. The ship was of a similar size and shape as the Jenny's Revenge and was busily dropping sails so as to match their own speed. She had no idea if this ship was their intended target as she knew not the ship's name. What she did know was that even if this was not L'Olonnais, they were still pirates and they would feel their wrath for daring to attacking the Jenny. She decided to risk staying above decks for a while longer to see the crew of the pirate vessel. Hunkering down to the ship's rails so as not to stand out, she aimed her spyglass towards their half deck knowing that whoever was in command of the ship would most likely be stood there. It didn't take long before she could make out the crew and only a short while later, she could actually see their faces clearly. Suddenly her skin prickled with goose bumps and her spine turned to ice. There he was, L'Olonnais, his gaunt stature gave a sharpness to the rest of his features, accented by his pencil moustache and pointy beard. Even at this distance and through a spyglass there was no escaping the cruel intent in the man's eyes. Thinking that she had already risked to much by remaining on deck for as long as she had, Mary bolted for the door which led below. As she did she turned to Lucy and the rest of the decoy party. She hoped that she would see them all again but felt that she should say something in case this turned out to be her last chance. "This is it ladies, Give them everything you have. I love you all."

Mary had no idea why she had said the last statement but then realised that she did love them, and the rest of the crew. They were her family now and she would do anything for them. Upon entering the gun deck, she was silently greeted by the crew there and their faces all wore the same question, is it him? She nodded sagely and was pleased to see that every one of them took on an air of grim determination, ready to settle the promise Mary had made to Anup Rai.

# Chapter seventeen.

*Blunderbuss: a short wide-muzzled firearm of the 17th century, used to fire shot with a scattering effect at close range.*

$\mathcal{L}$'Olonnais ship was now alongside the Jenny's Revenge and within boarding distance. The men looked confused to be seeing well dressed women on the upper deck instead of the Spanish sailors they had obviously expected. It was L'olonnais himself who broke the silence between the two vessels when in French he cried out, "Where is the crew?"

"Sorry Sir," Lucy replied. "I don't understand what you are saying."

She said all this in her best effort English upper-class accent as Ms. Jones had taught her, knowing that if the French Pirate detected her Spanish accent, his hatred for them would spell their death.

"Your crew."

L'Olonnais ask once again but this time in English, and clearly intrigued by the sight that laid before him.

"Where are your crew?"

"They became ill Sir." Lucy answered. "We are all that remains."

"Ill?" the pirate questioned. "Do they remain on board?"

"No Sir. We, that is the crew at first and then ourselves, threw them over the side when they passed away."

As she answered Lucy added little sobbing noises at the mention of death.

"We continued to do so till only we remained."

At this last statement L'olonnais and his crew exchanged glances and, just as Smith and his crew had, their body language became a chorus of lust.

"Sir," Lucy called out to the pirate Captain. "I beseech you. Would you help a lady in distress?"

As she spoke the rest of the decoy party slowly got into position. They moved into pairs along the rails of the Jenny, looking at once vulnerable but alluring at the same time as Anne had shown them.

"Captain!"

One of the pirates shouted barely able to contain his lustful excitement.

"We should help them!"

"Yeah!" Came another voiced. "We should go over an' give 'em what they need!"

More clapped and cheered at this last suggestion.

"Oui." L'Olonnais agreed. "Let us board this vessel and offer ourselves to these fine ladies."

No sooner had the words left the Captains mouth then the boarding ropes were thrown, their grappling hooks biting into the rails of the Jenny. As the two ships came closer together Lucy and her party put on a show of their relief and gratitude. Some bit their lower lip whilst others waved, and with each gesture the pirates before them became more worked up. None of them recognised the threat before them. No sooner had the boarding planks touched down to bridge the gap between the two ships then feet were upon them, their owners eager to feast upon what lay in front them. As those feet reached the halfway point the girls at the rails braced themselves, bent forward and brought their secreted arms to bear. The loads that erupted from the Blunderbusses was as destructive as their report was thunderous. Those closest to the Jenny who, mere seconds before had been traversing the boarding planks, were turned into chum in an instant. As the lethal projectiles spread out on their travels tearing through man and sail alike the girls at the rails exchanged places with those behind them and unleashed hell once more. Those foolish enough not to have taken cover or were in the belief that there was only to be a single volley were decimated by the second wave. With the deafening ring of the Blunderbusses in ears the decoy party dove to the relative safety of the ships sides making way for the Jenny's own boarding party, who now flooded onto the upper deck, Muskets primed and ready to take out any who had survived the horror of the

Blunderbuss. Those hiding out of sight may have truly believed that they were safe as they readied to counterattack. Any such thoughts were quickly torn away with their ship as the Jenny's cannon song gave chorus. Chain shot flew up through the decks shredding everything before it including the mainmast which toppled, almost in slow motion, into the foremast only coming to rest as the rigging of the two entwined it. As the crew of the Jenny starred at the ballet of the two masts, all jumped in surprise as the pirate ships far side blew out in a cloud of splinters as those cannons aimed at the water line added to the symphony of death. All who stood on the upper deck then watched, completely mesmerised as the pirate ship started to slip beneath the waves. So enwrapped in the scene before them were they that when the flaming figure of L'Olonnais swung from the mizzen mast of his own ship to the half deck of the Jenny's Revenge, he went almost unnoticed. As the pirate landed, he drew his cutlass and looked like the visage of the Grim Reaper himself, so twisted with rage was his face that it truly resembled a screaming skull. His hair and clothes smoldered as if he were a living representation of his dying ship. He strode to the nearest woman, cutlass raised intent on bringing it down in an overhead slash to cleave her in two. Isabel was the only one who had seen him and with two loping strides intercepted the pirates blow with her musket. With one hand clasping the butt and the other on the barrel, she arrested the blade before it could do any harm, but the sheer force of his blow drove her to her knees and very nearly chopped the rifle in two. Realizing that he had the advantage L'Olonnais pressed down on his cutlass his spare hand going to the back off the blade to give extra leverage.

The two combatants were evenly matched for strength, but the pirate had the upper hand in position.

A grin spread across L'Olonnais face, and he leaned over

Isabel, bringing his face into hers to ensure he could be heard over the din of his dying ship. He looked her in the eye and calmly all matter of fact said,

"Now bitch, you will die."

Seeing this as her only chance to try and regain control of the fight, Isabel spat in her adversary's face. The ploy worked and L'olonnais eased off, just a fraction, but it was enough for Isabel to adjust her grip on her rifle and get her feet back underneath her. She wouldn't have believed it possible but L'olonnais looked more infuriated than ever. With a strength fueled by shear fury he bore down on his blade once more and was greeted by a crack from Isabel's rifle as it began to break under the pressure. Again he lent in putting his face to hers, the smell of burnt hair and flesh almost making Isabel gag.

"When this is over."

The enraged pirate told her, his voice unnervingly calm.

"I shall cut off your face and wear it as my own."

Truly disturbed by the man's words Isabel pushed at his cutlass but as she did so her rifle rotated in her grip causing her to pull the trigger. The weapon that she had so carefully primed to ensure that it wouldn't misfire now went off right in their faces. Both gladiators parted at the flash from the gunpowder. Isabel who had taken the brunt of the blast fell to the deck clutching at her face, howling with pain. L'olonnais who had merely been dazzled by the flash, stumbled back towards the ship's rails, blinking wildly in an attempt to clear his vision. This gave the rest of the crew on deck the opportunity they needed. With Isabel safely out of the way three of the boarding party opened fire, their aim true, all three rounds hitting the man square in the chest. Not willing to take the risk that the crazy French pirate may have somehow survived the firing squad, yet another member of the boarding party charged forward blade in hand and with an almighty swing decapitated the man. Eyes finally clear of the effects of the flash, the last thing L'olonnais ever saw were the boots of his executioners as his head hit the deck of the Jenny's Revenge.

# Chapter eighteen.

Barber-surgeon: When King Charles 1 decreed that all ships sailing from British ports shall have a surgeon, the ships barber was charged with the task. Accustomed to the use of razors, they became the ships medical practitioner.

By the time Mary arrived on the upper deck, Isabel had entirety of the boarding and decoy parties surrounding her. "Clear the way for the Captain!"
Ms. Jones ordered as she emerged from below decks a few paces behind Mary. As the women parted Mary was able to see Isabel for the first time since the skirmish began. After the death of L'Olonnais a runner had been sent down to the Jenny's Captain to inform her of the dire situation. Her Master-at-Arms was still lying on the deck with her hands clasped to her face shrieking with pain. The muscular woman fought off all attempts to help her, so great was the pain. Mary turned to her First mate,
"We need to see the damage." she said grimly.
Ms. Jones looked to the boarding party and then down to the writhing form of Isabel.
"Hold her down."
She ordered, her tone showing no emotion, a clear indication to all around her that this was not open to debate. Three of the boarding party carried out the order. One straddled and pinned Isabel's legs whilst the other two grabbed her shoulders. Under normal circumstances the ship's Master-at-Arms would have been able to fight off the women with little effort but now, delirious with pain, she was able to be restrained. Mary knelt beside Isabel and with the same kind tone of voice that she had used when recruiting every member of the Jenny's crew, said to her friend.
"Isabel, it's me Mary. I know it hurts but I'm going to have to take a look your face."
Gently but firmly, she took Isabel's hands in her own and prised them away from their protective position over her face. What Mary saw took away not only her breath away, but all who were able to see the stricken Master-at-Arms. When her Musket had gone off it had been so close to Isabel's face that the powder charge flash had burned the

poor woman's left eye and the skin all around it. Isabel's natural reaction of clutching her hand to the pain had in fact been the worst thing she could have done. Where the very hottest part of the blast had hit, the skin had instantly blistered and when Isabel's hand had come into contact with them, they had burst adhering hand and face together. Much of the skin around the Master-at-Arms eye had come away when Mary had moved the woman's hands to inspect the damage.

"We need a doctor!"

Ms. Jones called out and then repeated the statement. The crew simply stared at the First mate in dumfounded. There was no Doctor aboard the Jenny's Revenge and Ms. Jones like the rest of the crew knew that only too well.

"Does anybody have any medical knowledge?"

Ms. Jones asked them.

"One of you must know something surely! Many of you were mothers and wives. Somebody must know enough to help!"

As she spoke the frustration she felt at the situation and her own helplessness started to creep into her voice. The call was echoed around the ship by the crew until two stepped forward. The cook was one but was excused due to the importance of her other duty. The other was a young Able rate.

"If you please, I know a little."

The girl said in sheepish tones.

"My sister suffered with the pox when we was young an' I 'ad to look after 'er.

When she was young! Mary thought, for the girl looked to be no more than seventeen, but she was all they had.

"Take her to my cabin!"

She ordered those around Isabel and then turned to address the girl who'd just volunteered to be her medic.

"What's your name girl?"

Mary asked, admonishing herself for not already knowing.
The girl stuttered at first but then replied in a soft London
accent,
"Rebecca Ma'am."
"Tell me what you need Rebecca and if we have it, it's
yours."
Mary told her then turned to her First mate.
"Ms. Jones. See to Rebecca and Isabel's needs and keep me
updated on the Master-at-Arms health."
Ms. Jones replied with a curt nod before guiding the
volunteer ships medic to the Captain's quarters.
"Helm! Navs!" Mary bellowed. "Plot me the quickest
course you can back to Port Royal!"
Anne found Mary sat at a table in what was now the Galley
and Mess Hall. Like many ships, the area below decks was
used for a number of things. Now that the battle between
L'Olonnais was over, the decks had been scrubbed, the
cannons stowed, and tables had been set for the evening
meal. Mary had her elbows pressed into the tabletop,
forehead cradled in her palms with her fingers entwined in
her hair. The stress the woman was feeling was palpable
and as Anne drew closer, she could hear her muttering to
herself.
"Captain, are you alright?"
She asked, her voice soft and soothing. Mary didn't look
up, but she did answer.
"I should have thought about it."
Her voice was harsh and chastising, but Anne could tell that
none of the bitterness in her Captains voice was directed at
her. No, all of the anger was directed inwards and it ate at
Mary like a ravenous shark.
Anne took the seat opposite Mary and reached out a hand
resting it gently upon the woman's arm.
"What should you 'ave thought of?"
At this question Mary did look up locking her gaze with the

Quartermasters, eyes blood shot and raw from angry tears.
"A doctor!" She growled.
"I should have thought of a doctor. Or a Nurse. At the very least I should have thought to bring someone with some knowledge of medicine at the very least!"
With her outburst over Mary returned her head to her hands, grasping great handfuls of hair so tightly Anne feared she meant to tear it out.
"I failed and now poor Isabel is in pain because of me."
"Isabel knew the risks when she agreed to join the crew." Anne told Mary, her voice firm and matter of fact.
"We all did. We know that every time we go out we might not be comin' back."
Reaching over, Anne gently took Mary's hands and pulled them from her hair to hold them firmly in her own.
"So you didn't think to bring along a doctor, t'aint the end of the world." She smiled at Mary with the one she reserved for those she really liked. "And anyway, turns out we got young Rebecca. She's done a fair job of patching up Isabel. Come on, let's go see 'er."
They found Isabel asleep in the cot in the Captain's quarters. Rebecca had made some make-shift bandages from a uniform shirt and almost all of the Master-at-Arm's head was bound. Only the right side of the woman's face remained visible and at peace as she slept. Rebecca sat beside her patient and turned towards the two as they entered the room.
"'Ow is she?" Anne asked, noting that Rebecca looked truly exhausted.
"Don't let her current peacefulness fool you."
The girl replied barely above a whisper, although Anne was unsure if this was how she always spoke or so as not to wake Isabel.

"She's so strong. I cleaned and bandaged 'er as best I could an' she stayed with me the 'hole time. Even with nuthin' to dull the pain."

Mary looked down at the deck, unable to look Rebecca in the eye. It was true that they had no medicines aboard, but they also had no Rum or the likes with them either. She had wanted to keep the temptation of alcohol away from the crew. It had never crossed her mind that it could be used for other purposes.

"In future," Mary addressed the girl directly now, strong and firm, but still with an air of humility.

"You will have all that you need."

"I don't understand," Rebecca replied with obvious confusion.

"What future, an' what will I be needin'?"

Mary squared herself off and locked eyes with Rebecca.

"You are to be our ship's Barber-surgeon," she informed the girl.

"You will be provisioned with all the best books…."

Mary paused mid flow and considered.

"You can read?" she asked.

Rebecca nodded that she could and so Mary continued.

"As I said, you will be provisioned with the best medical books and medicines that we can get. We will also find you someone to learn from and when the ship is in harbour, you will spend your time with them."

For the first time since the attack on L'Olonnais, Mary smiled pleased with her decision.

"What say you Rebecca?"

Anne asked the newly appointed Barber.

"Thank you Ma'am!"

The girl replied seemingly pleased with her new role.

"I'll do me best to learn all I can!"

With her confidence boosted both women noted that the girl's voice came out stronger and louder.

"How is it that you come to be with us?"
Mary asked. She normally did the recruiting but couldn't recall having done so with Rebecca.

"I'm an orphan." The girl said matter-of-factly. "Ms. Jones recruited me."

That, Mary thought, explained why she didn't recognise this particular member of the crew.

"She caught me pick pocketing a couple of gents and followed me back to where I was hiding out."

"And that's when Ms. Jones asked you to join us?" Anne asked.

"Yes miss. Ms. Jones said I had good hands and would make an excellent crewman."

"And you sister?" Mary quizzed the girl. "Did she join the crew with you?"

"Oh no Captain. She never survived the pox."

# Chapter nineteen.

Port Royal: located in the mouth of Kingston Harbour, it became known as the most wicked and sinful city in the world. Famous for its pirate population the Governors turned a blind eye to their activities, this was in part due to the great wealth they bought with them. Port Royal was once considered to be one of the wealthiest cities in the world.

By the time they pulled into Port Royal it was obvious that despite Rebecca's best efforts, Isabel's injury had become infected. For the moments in time that the woman had gained consciousness were filled with delirious ramblings or violence. Once, while Rebecca was changing her dressings, Isabel had come to and struck out at the girl. The blow was so hard it had sent the young Barber-surgeon sprawling across the Captain's cabin. Believing that Rebecca was responsible for the pain she was in, Isabel dived on the girl lying prone before her and rained down blow after blow before passing out from the effort. After that Rebecca refused to attend to her patient without a guard, and nobody could blame her.

Once they had dropped anchor, Mary sent Lucy to find a Doctor with the cover story that it was for her husband. As one of the few members of the crew who had no facial flaws, it was believed that most in Port Royal would believe her over those on the crew who bore the scars of their treatment by the hands of pirates. Mary also believed that it would be easier to bring the Doctor to the ship, than Isabel to the Doctor, though It did run the risk of revealing the secret that the Jenny's Revenge had an all-female crew. Be they pirate hunters or merchants, women at sea as anything other than as passengers simply didn't happen. Mary was confident though that their identity would remain as a secret, as in a place like Port Royal silence could be bought as easily as Rum. Especially if the coins purchasing the vow continued to flow. If the Doctor that Lucy returned with turned out to be skilled enough, she would see to it that Rebecca would apprentice with him, and the promise of a heavy purse should be more than enough to secure his services.

When Lucy returned, the man she presented to her Captain was short and pudgy. His jowled cheeks were permanently flushed suggesting that the man was either incredibly unfit or partook in a drink far too often to be good for his health. Mary decided it was probably both. She greeted the Doctor with a handshake.

"Good day Sir."

Her tone was formal but friendly.

"I'm Captain Mary of the Jenny's Revenge, and who do I have the pleasure of meeting?"

The night before they reached Port Royal, she and Ms. Jones had agreed that Mary should act and speak as though she were born into this way of life. The equal to all who set foot aboard her fine vessel. Ms. Jones had been present on many an occasion when her husband had attended this function or that as a Lieutenant in the Royal Navy. So she schooled the Captain of the Jenny's Revenge, all be it at the rush, in the ways of etiquette.

If nothing else, it was one more layer of the disguise that hid who they really were.

"Good day to you madam."

The Doctor said somewhat pompously, his voice reedy and nasally.

"My name is Avery Smith."

As he spoke his eyes darted nervously around the room taking in everything and everyone as if assessing where the next threat was going to come from. His handshake, Mary noted with some confusion, was as if belonging to a completely different person to the one that stood before her. It was firm, confident and steady. That of a skilled surgeon and it was as if, Mary thought, Doctor Avery Smith were two separate people rolled into one. Avery Smith the man seemed easily intimidated, scared of his own shadow, someone used to being bullied. Avery Smith the Doctor, or at least according to the man's hands, was precise and confident.

Used to making life or death decisions.

Mary also noted that his eyes would linger a little bit longer on certain members of her crew even as the victim in him was looking for a way to escape. All of these traits Mary knew could be used to exploit the man, after all, it wasn't just coin that could be used to buy a man's silence or services.

"Come Doctor Smith. There's a member of the crew the Captain wishes you to look at." Anne said.

She didn't introduce herself just simply indicated that the Doctor was to follow her.

Avery looked to Mary, but she had already turned her back on him and started to walk away.

"Don't you be worrying none Doctor Smith. The Captain will be wanting a word with you later."

Anne told the man in a manner that, although not abrupt or menacing, left no room for argument. The Quartermaster led the Doctor to the Captain's cabin and after opening the door for him said,

"In 'ere if you will Doctor Smith. You'll be aided by Miss Rebecca and she'll be introducing you to your patient."

"And you? Where will you be Miss......"

The Doctor left the sentence open expecting Anne to fill in the missing details. She simply levelled her gaze at him.

"I'll be waiting out 'ere for you."

She told him, her tone flat and unemotional.

"To take you back to the Captain when yer done."

Although Anne hadn't said as much there was no doubt in Avery's mind as to the meaning behind the woman's words. I'll be standing guard right here, so don't try anything. Once inside the cabin Avery was surprised at how well-lit it was. All of the windows were uncovered, and oil lamps had been placed in the areas that the natural light failed to reach.

As promised the Doctor was greeted by Rebecca who did indeed introduce him to his patient. In the quiet of the Captain's quarters, with no one to intimidate him, and the only eyes to cast judgment on him coming from a single source Avery was able to relax and let his professional side come to the surface. He spoke as he went about his business, narrating his every move.

"Hmmm. The patient's injuries have been dressed, crudely but none the less effectively."

He looked to Rebecca and inclined his headfirst towards Isabel and then back to Rebecca. She nodded enthusiastically.

"Yes Sir. I made 'em from a shirt."

Her voice was barely audible even in the quite of the cabin.

"No need to whisper."

Isabel said startling both Rebecca and the Doctor.

"I'm not asleep."

"Not whispering."

Rebecca retorted, her voice strong but still quiet. Avery presumed that this was how the girl always spoke. He turned to look at Isabel and instantly judged by the glazing of the woman's one uncovered eye, that this bout of consciousness would only be fleeting, so took the opportunity to ask as much as he could while he had the opportunity.

"How exactly did you come to be in need of my services?"

"Musket. Accident."

Isabel answered, her words broken. The effort of talking though the pain was etched upon what could be seen of her face.

"A musket accident you say!"

Avery's curiosity was peaked.

"What in God's name were you doing with a musket?"

Even in her present condition Isabel was careful with her answers. She also knew she had to divulge just enough of the truth to make her words believable.

"Practicing. In case of pirates."

The Master-at-Arms croaked.

"Didn't pack the charge right. Went off in my face."
Took out some of your teeth too, Avery thought noticing
the gaps in the woman's mouth. To her face he asked
"Why dear lady would you need to be practicing for
anything, let alone pirates!"
Although he drew short of actually laughing, both of the
women heard the incredulity in the man's tone.
"We intend to set sail one day mesure!"
Her words were suddenly strong and steady, bolstered by
anger. That this weasel of a man could presume to be able
to pass judgment on anyone, let alone her or any member of
their crew. She sat up so better to look the man in the eye.
"Calm yourself mademoiselle."
The Doctor said bringing up his hands palm out to support
his words.
"I meant no. It's just…."
He paused and looked from one woman to the other.
"You do realise that it's bad luck for a woman to be aboard
a vessel at sea?"
"Superstition and poppycock!"
Rebecca exclaimed and Avery was surprised by the volume
of the girl's voice. It would appear that she can be heard
over the breeze when her heckles are raised he thought.
Turning his attention back to Isabel, he discovered that the
woman's outburst had taken its toll and cost her her
consciousness. Oh well he thought, it was probably for the
best as he needed to take off her bandages and assess the
extent of her injuries. Turning to Rebecca Avery asked for
warm water and a clean cloth. As she in turn conveyed his
request with the woman outside the door, the Doctor started
the task of removing the makeshift bandages.
The smell was unbelievable, and each layer of bandage
removed only served to intensify the fetid stench, as if he
were peeling a decomposing onion. Even the Doctor with
all of his experience dealing with some of the lowest forms

of villainy, and the inflictions they regularly bought before him baulked as the last of bandages came away revealing the extent of the infection. Although Rebecca had obviously been cleaning the wound regularly, infection, probably from the gun powder left in it had set into the eye itself and Avery confirmed as much to Rebecca when she returned with the water he had requested. He admitted to himself that he was quite impressed that the girl didn't blanch or turn away from the sight of her friend's face, nor did she gag at the smell.

"I'm afraid your friend is going to have to lose her eye."

Avery pointed to poor Isabel's face and started his narrative once more.

"The eye itself has become swollen with infection judging by its colour. I suspect the poor woman has already lost the sight in it."

Rebecca placed the water down beside Isabel's head and made her own inspection of the eye. The Doctor hadn't been exaggerating when he said that the eye had become swollen. It had started to push its way out of the socket, the eyelid no longer being able to contain it. Now that the bandages had been removed the damaged orb was able to weep freely its buildup of puss.

"What are we going to do?"

Rebecca questioned the Doctor.

'We' thought Avery amused by the statement. You put on a dressing and now you think you're ready to be a surgeon! To her face ho told her how they would have to remove the eye and sew shut the eyelid.

He instructed her to wash her hands and then clean her friends face. In the meantime he went to his bag and removed the instruments needed to perform the operation, and an eye patch. Seeing the patch Rebecca raised a questioning eyebrow.

"You'd be surprised how many I give out on a regular basis."

The procedure was rather simple Rebecca thought afterwards. To remove the eye the Doctor had used what looked like a plain old spoon. He then got Rebecca to cut the cord at the back of the eye before he plopped the pustulous orb unceremoniously into the bowl of water. Then he pushed the cord back into the now empty socket and sewed the lid shut with stitches so neat a seamstress could have done no better. When he had finished he washed his hands in the same water he'd just dropped the eye into and then handed the eye patch to Rebecca.

"She'll be to tender for this for a while, but once the pain has eased and she gets a look at herself, I imagine she'll be grateful for it."

"Is there anything we can give her for the pain?"

Rebecca asked tentatively already knowing the answer but wanting to hear it from a real Doctor.

"I suggest a good strong Rum,"

The Doctor advised.

"If you can find any, I hear willow bark can be effective." The tree bark had been used by the ancient Greeks to some effect but the look on the Doctor's face said it all, good luck trying to find some in these waters. Realising his job here was done Avery Smith once more took on the air of a victim, his posture changing to that of a man easily intimidated, as if he'd just donned an extremely heavy coat.

"I believe your Captain wanted to see me when I'd finished?"

Rebecca nodded and knocked on the door. It opened and there stood Anne.

"All done?"

She asked, and after receiving a nod from the both of them said in a cheerful voice,

"Excellent. If you'd follow me Doctor, I'll be takin' you to see the Captain."

The Doctor was then escorted to the main hold where a makeshift meeting room had been set up. There were a couple of chairs, simple but comfortable, facing each other with a small table holding a bottle and cups placed between them. One of the chairs was occupied by the Captain and when Avery came close enough she invited him to sit with her with a simple hand gesture.

"How is your patient?"

Mary asked, eager for news of Isabel but careful to make it seem as if she were simply asking after one of her crew. Avery replied as he sat.

"She had to lose the eye I'm afraid. But I'm sure she will make a full recovery."

"You're *sure* she'll make a full recovery?"

Mary's question was edged with menace. She wanted something a little more solid than 'sure'.

"I assure you Captain."

The Doctor squeaked.

"I've done that procedure a dozen times! I know what I'm doing."

"But…"

Mary leaned forward placing her hands on her knees and locking her gaze with Avery's.

"It's down to the patient. If she wants to recover, she will."

With that Mary leaned back in her chair.

"Excellent news Doctor,"

She said in a jovial manner.

"Could I interest you in a glass of Port?"

She picked up the bottle from the table and removed the stopper. Avery nodded vigorously. He'd never tried the wine before but had heard that members of the Royal Navy gentry often drank it. Unbeknownst to him, this was exactly the reason that Mary now had this particular drink onboard.

She poured two cups and passed one to the Doctor before relaxing back into her chair and taking a long draw of the wine into her mouth. Avery watched the procession with great interest and once satisfied that the drink wasn't poisoned, gulped from his own cup.

"Doctor I have a proposition for you."

Avery stopped slurping from his cup, his eyes darting around the room. Normally when someone started a conversation like so in Port Royal it meant death to the person receiving the proposal.

"Relax Doctor."

Mary said in a chirpy tone.

"I have need for your trade and you will be paid for it."

Avery's eyebrows arched in surprise at the Captain's statement and his curiosity peaked he asked,

"How may I be of assistance?"

Mary replied with a question of her own.

"How did you find young Miss Rebecca? Did she keep her head whilst you worked on her crew mate?"

Somewhat puzzled the Doctor replied,

"Yes. She didn't wince or shy away once. Not even when I pried the patient eye out."

"Excellent news Doctor for my proposal is this. Take Miss Rebecca on as your apprentice. Whenever we are in port she will work for you and I will pay you for the liberty."

"So, I get an apprentice and paid good money for it!"

A smile spread across the Doctors weaselly features.

"I accept your proposal Captain!"

He offered his cup up for a refill.

"Let's drink to it."

# Chapter twenty.

The pirate's eye patch: Commonly believed to be used to cover up a missing eye, it was also used as an early form of night vision. The patch would be placed over an eye whilst above decks and then removed when below where poor lighting made it hard to see. The now uncovered eye would then be able to see in the darkened interior of the ship.

For the next few months, the Jenny's Revenge operated solely as a merchant vessel. She operated only short haul so as not to draw attention as a target for pirates, and whenever they were back in Port Royal Rebecca would spend her time with Doctor Smith learning her trade. This break from their mission allowed Isabel to adjust to having just the one eye. When she had recovered from her surgery, the Master-at-Arms had had the most horrendous mood swings and, as before, they ranged from feeling utterly worthless to extreme violent anger. Just as before Mary had to put her friend under watch, but this time it was not only for the safety of the crew but for Isabel's too. During her lowest points she had become suicidal at times and Mary felt that she would lose her friend to depression. At the other end of the scale, when she became violent there were few aboard the Jenny that could calm the Master-at-Arms and Mary was worried that if left unchecked, she might lose more than just the one member of the ship's company. That had lasted six or seven days and even though Isabel had come to terms with her affliction, she now harboured more hatred for pirates than any other member of the crew, even Mary herself. Seeking out her friend Mary found her in the ship's armoury. As she entered Isabel looked up from her inspection of one of the Blunderbusses. Mary froze dead in her tracks, eyes wide with fear. The vision she was greeted with was that of death. Isabel had removed her patch and darkened the hollows of her eyelid and the cheek below it with soot, giving that side of her face the appearance of a skull.

"Sorry Captain!"

Isabel gasped seeing the reaction her visage had upon her friend.

"I have been experimenting on ways to bring fear into the hearts of our enemies."

"I would say that you have succeeded in that matter."

Mary replied still not looking Isabel in the face.

"If you would please put the patch on and come into the light of the day."

Isabel did as she was asked, replacing her patch and wiping the soot from her face on her sleeve as she accompanied Mary up onto the upper deck.

"It does you no good to keep moping around below decks." Mary told her friend when they got into the fresh air.

"But my eye and behavior."

Isabel mumbled clearly ashamed of both.

"We all have our scars to bare."

Mary told her absent mindedly rubbing at her disfigured nose.

"And as for the crew, they would forgive you for just about anything. After all you took on L'Olonnais one on one to protect them."

A slight smile crossed the French woman's lips, but she turned away quickly in case she exposed her broken teeth. Instead she pretended to be taking in the view of the harbour. As she looked out across the water, she noticed a row boat making its way towards them.

"Quartermaster!" she bellowed. "Quartermaster!"

The call was echoed around the ship and before long Anne appeared on the upper deck. She spotted Isabel and rushed over.

"Do we have anybody ashore?"

The Master-at-Arms asked, her French accent making it hard for the woman to understand with the speed the question came out. Anne paused as she tried to discern the words. Her eyes followed the path indicated by Isabel's pointing hand and finally she understood what she had been asked.

"Only Rebecca's ashore at the moment, but she's not due back for a few hours."

Mary had pulled out her spyglass and was getting a better

look at the approaching boat and its occupant.

"It's definitely Rebecca," she confirmed. "And by the looks of it she's returning with some urgency. Are we ready to set sail Quartermaster?"

"Yes Ma'am. We just secured the latest cargo Ms. Jones returned with. That's where I was when you called for me."

"Good, I believe we may have need to."

As Rebecca climbed on to the deck it was quite obvious that something wasn't right. The girl's hands and dress were covered with blood. As the rest of the crew busied themselves preparing the Jenny to be able to sail as soon as the tide allowed, Mary ushered Rebecca into her cabin closely followed by Ms. Jones.

"What happened?"

Mary asked as she directed the girl to one of the chairs around the cabins table. Both Mary and Ms. Jones tried to stay as quiet as possible as they knew that when it came, Rebecca's explanation would be little more than a whisper. Rebecca stared at the blood on her hands and dress and then to her Captain.

"I killed him."

She stated cold and flat.

"Doctor Avery. I killed him."

Both Mary and Ms. Jones stared at the girl totally taken aback before looking at each other. Each could see that the other had come to the same conclusion that the mess the girl was in was due to some procedure gone wrong. Neither had expected her to say what she just had. Ms. Jones grabbed the cup and bottle that sat on the table and poured the contents from one to the other. She then placed the cup into the girl's hands and instructed her to drink.

"Tell us exactly what happened." she asked softly.

Rebecca sniffed the contents of the cup and found it contained Rum, and after a few seconds gulped it down.

"He was alright at first, Doctor Avery that is, and seemed pleased that he 'ad someone to help 'im. He taught me all manner of stuff and I learned a lot. It was on the third or fourth time I went to work for 'im that things got weird. He told me to tie me hair up so it wouldn't be in the way when working, though he'd been fine with it before. Then when I was with a patient he'd 'ave to be right behind me, said it was so he could get a proper view, from a Doctors perspective, but I swear I caught him sniffing me a couple of times. I should've said something then, but like I said he was teachin' me so much and I knew that we needed a Barber-surgeon, so I let it go. And blokes are always trying it on. Should've said something' though coz then his hands started to wander. A little brush 'ere and there at first but coz I didn't call 'im on it he must of thought it was okay coz he got more familiar."

Rebecca paused in her recounting and indicated that more Rum would be needed to continue. Cup filled and drained once more she continued.

"Last night he tried to take it all the way. After the last patient 'ad left he pressed me up against the surgery table as I was cleaning up. His hands were all over as I wriggled to get free. Stop I told 'im stop and he looks at me all confused. But you want me he says. You let me touch you. I should 'ave told you to stop then I said. But you were teaching me so much. His face reddend at that, so embarrassed was he. I said it was alright but then he looks at me all angry and says you do want me! He then grabbed me by the 'air and pushed me face into the table. He starts pulling up my skirt but can't do it with one hand. He forgot though that I 'adn't finished cleaning up. There was a scalpel still on the table, so I grabbed it and swung it around blindly behind me. He screamed and let me go and when I turned to look at 'im, he 'ad blood staining his shirt where I'd caught 'im.

He then comes at me, snarling and enraged. I still 'ad the scalpel though so I lashed out with it. Lashed out with it and slashed his throat."

Ms. Jones knelt beside Rebecca and placed a hand gently on her knee.

"You did the right thing girl. It was self defence. But, if I may ask, what have you been doing between now and then?"

"I've been cleaning up the mess I made."

Rebecca said earnestly.

"Over the past few weeks it's not just surgery and the likes I've been learning.

Old Doctor Smith 'as been visited by all walks of life but he's 'ad more than a few pirates come in to get sorted out. So I made it look as if one of them 'ad come in and weren't 'appy with their treatment."

"You covered your tracks. Wise girl."

Ms. Jones said nodding her approval at Rebecca's handling of the situation.

"What about you?" Mary asked. "Won't people be suspicious that the Doctors dead and you've gone missing?"

"Not really Ma'am," Rebecca replied. " Because I weren't always there, people got used to my coming an' going."

"Very well."

Mary said, satisfied with the logic in the girls answer.

She was annoyed at herself though that Rebecca had had to face such an ordeal. Annoyed that once again she had placed her trust in a man, a supposedly trustworthy man this time, who had hidden who he really was.

"Ms. Jones is right, you handled the situation well."

She told the girl and Rebecca seemed to perk up from the praise that the two had given her.

"But I feel it would be prudent to set sail and put a bit of distance between ourselves and Port Royal for a while."

Ms. Jones nodded in agreement and Rebecca felt compelled to join in.

# Chapter twenty-one.

Letter of marque: A government licence that authorised a private person such as a privateer or corsair to attack and capture the vessels of a nation at war with the issuer.

The Jenny's Revenge set sail as soon as the afternoon's tide allowed, heading for the Spanish Main. The plan was to head along the coast stopping at various ports with the ultimate destination of Old Panama City. Their cargo consisted of smoked meats, popular with sailors around the Caribbean due to its long life. The meats had first been introduced into the area by French settlers. They smoked the various meats over a small wooden platform called a Boucan giving the meat the name Viande boucanee or jerked meat. Those selling the meat soon became known as Boucanieres. Ironically when trade came to the area many of these Boucanieres went out of business and needed to find a new line of work. Now referred to by many as Buccaneers, the onetime meat traders like many others down on their luck turned to a life of piracy.

Whilst looking to procure provisions for the Jenny, Ms. Jones had discovered that there was still a market for jerky along the Spanish Main and had secured some for their latest cargo. Although the distance to the main wasn't too great, with fair winds and calm seas they could make it in three or four days, Mary figured that with the time spent in trading and the return trip it would allow for sufficient time for Rebecca's incident with Avery Smith to be forgotten about. After all, in a city of sodomy such as Port Royal, the murder of a little-known doctor wouldn't even reach the ears of the Governor. Towards the end of the second day, smoke could be seen on the horizon. Even through her spyglass Mary could make out little. Judging by the amount of smoke hanging in the air, she could tell that the fire that produced it was of a considerable size.

It was nearing dusk when the Jenny's Revenge drew with in distance of the port town of Chagre on the Spanish Main. Mary had decided to drop anchor preferring to dock in the light of the following day. All through that day they had seen smoke hazing the air, but it had grown thin and Mary presumed it was simply just from farmers burning their fields. She was about to give the order to drop anchor when the lookout spotted sails. She pulled out her spyglass but couldn't make out much as the light was dim and the ship was running dark and with minimum sails so as to reduce the noise of the rigging. Mary continued to watch, and it soon became clear to her that the ship was trying to slip away unnoticed. Her mind was instantly made up, they had to be pirates. No other type of ship would feel the need to sail under such conditions. She had no clue as to who the Captain of this vessel was, but it had been a long time since their last encounter with pirates, and she felt now was as good a time as any to resume their vendetta. Unfortunately, as they hadn't expected to run into any trouble the cannons were all stowed and in this light the decoy party would be all but unseen so they would have to rely solely on their boarding party. Decision made she turned to the crew and started to issue orders.

"Helm! I want you to take a wide berth of that ship and then swing around to come in on their port side."

"Will we be able to catch them with such a maneuver?" Amy's muted, throaty question floated out of the gloom.

"They are under minimal sails to our full."

Mary grinned at the girl.

"We'll be able to catch them alright!"

Next she sent word for the boarding party to make ready. Within minutes they were on deck and Mary could see that they had all taken from Isabel's lead. Every member of the boarding party had blackened their eyes and cheeks with soot giving them a horrific skull like visage in the waning light.

"What is the plan Captain?"

Isabel asked and Mary noted that she had taken her eye patch off.

"I know we've never done anything like this before but we're going to take a leaf out of L'Olonnais book, Mary explained. Isabel looked at her Captain quizzically.

"We're going to board that vessel as we come along side by swinging down from the rigging."

Mary explained. Isabel's face brightened with the realisation that they would get to try something daring and new. From Mary's point of view the Master-at-Arms looked even more terrifying when happy.

"Once aboard we'll rush the Captain and hope that his crew surrenders."

It was a textbook pirate maneuver which Mary hoped would give them the advantage. As they came around the stern of the ship, they could just make out its name in the moon light.

"The Satisfaction."

Lucy whispered surprising Mary as she hadn't realised the head of the decoy party had come up on deck.

"Captain I need to be on the boarding party."

The Spanish woman demanded.

"That is the ship that destroyed my village."

Mary nodded recognising the woman's desire for revenge. She had been given the opportunity to kill the monster who had destroyed her life and now Lucy had the chance to do the same.

"You have until we're alongside to make ready."

She called after the woman as she raced below deck, but Mary knew that she would be. As they pulled alongside Mary was as surprised to see that only the helmsman was on the upper deck as he was to see them.

Before he could raise an alarm, a crossbow bolt pierced his neck killing him in an instant.

Mary turned to see Anne, crossbow in hand stood on the half deck and nodded her thanks to the woman. A moment later Mary, Isabel, Lucy and the boarding party had swung

122

across and stood on the deck of the Satisfaction, weapons at the ready. In the silence they could hear revelry coming from below decks but with far fewer voices than expected. Quickly and quietly, they descended below decks before storming the main hold where the crew sat laughing and drinking. Two of them were taken out by pistol shot to show them that Mary and her crew meant business.

"What the hell is this?"

Boomed out the voice of Henry Morgan, his Welsh accent thick under the influence of drink. The Captain of the Satisfaction got to his feet and stared at the women who had interrupted his celebrations. Mary was surprised to find Morgan's crew consisted of just enough men to operate the ship. Unbeknownst to her, if they had arrived just a few days earlier, the situation would have been a very different story. Until recently Morgan had been in command of thirty ships and around fourteen hundred men. They had set out to raid the Spanish Main with Panama being the main their target. Morgan had decided that the best way to attack the city was overland, but the Spanish had gotten word of the pirate's intensions and had moved all of their gold, silver and even their cattle so as to leave nothing for the invaders. Even with all the preparations and heavily outnumbering their invaders, Panamá had fallen. Morgan was furious that the plunder from such a hard-won expedition was so small and had set Panama ablaze in an attempt to ransom more from his captives, but to no avail. On his return trip to Chagre, Morgan and a selection of his most loyal crew had made away with the spoils, leaving the rest of his fleet to the mercy of the Spanish.

"Sir! You are guilty of acts of piracy and we are here for justice!"

Mary announced.

"Piracy!" The Welshman scoffed. "Madam, I am no pirate."

"YOU KILLED MY FAMILY AND BURNED MY VILLAGE!"

Lucy screamed and had to be restrained by Isabel as she tried to bring her pistol to aim.

"Ah, Spanish I take it. Well dear lady we are at war with the Spanish, and I have a letter of marque from the Governor of Port Royal himself! That makes us privateers, not pirates."

There was a flurry of movement from behind them and both Morgan and Mary moved to see what it was. One of Morgan's crew had made the mistake of thinking he could get the drop on one of Mary's boarding party. The mistaken man now lay on the deck with the blade of a Katar buried up to the hilt in his chest.

"I repeat Sir, you are guilty of piracy."

Mary repeated her opening statement returning her full attention to Morgan.

"Or have you not heard, the English are at peace with Spain and your 'letter' is worth nothing."

"And I stand by my statement that I am a king's sanctioned privateer!" Morgan said but his bluster had ebbed, replaced by uncertainty.

"If, and I do mean if," he went on. "I am guilty I will be arrested and hung when I return to Port Royal."

Mary considered this and the letter of marque. She knew many had been given a letter, normally from the local Governor, allowing them to legally conduct raids against the Spanish. This meant that if she were to execute this man and his crew, and the letter was still valid, then she and her crew could be found guilty of crimes against the crown.

"I will allow you and your crew to continue to Port Royal where you will undoubtedly face justice for your crimes." She said begrudgingly.

"WHAT!"

Lucy screamed once more, outraged at what she was

hearing.

"What about our vendetta? My people? He deserves to die!"

Raising her voice so all in the hold could hear Mary announced,

"We have no choice. If this man and his crew are still under the protection of the crown with their letter of marque, we will be made enemies of England."

She turned the full attention of her gaze back on Morgan and it blazed into his.

"Mark my words Sir."

She said her voice low and thick with menace.

"If you do not find justice at the hang man's gallows on your return, Kings Man or not, I will be back for you."

Back onboard the Jenny, Mary and her crew watched as the Satisfaction sailed into the moonlight and Fire burned within Mary's guts that she had been forced to let them go.

# Chapter twenty-two.

Galleon: a large three-masted, multi-decked sailing ships used especially by the Spanish between the 15th and 18th centuries and were the principal vessels drafted for use as warships.

Lucy had been correct Mary thought. They should be thinking about their vendetta. They had set out to kill any pirates they could find but with the injury Isabel had gained during their encounter with L'Olonnais, they had taken a break. A break Mary now feared had gone on for too long. She realised that they had unwittingly become their own cover story, merchant sailors. As soon as Captain Morgan had sailed out of distance Mary had ordered the Jenny to anchor in a secluded bay. The following day she had called a council of her head staff to meet in the Captain's cabin. Sat around the table were the First mate, Master-at-Arms, Quartermaster and the head of the decoy party. Lucy sat in silence but glared daggers at her Captain.

"Ladies."

Mary said from her place at the head of the table.

"Last night Lucy was correct. We have neglected the very reason that we are here for and in doing so have betrayed those we sort justice for."

Lucy's gaze lost some of its venom with Mary's statement but stayed locked in place. The other women at the table looked to each other and nodded in agreement.

"What do you propose?" Isabel asked.

"I've been consulting with Ms. Jones and have shown her what our land crew have been gathering. From that information we have made a list of those that we will hunt down."

A wave of excitement rippled around the room. All of the women present and no doubt the whole, crew were eager to get back to the reason they had signed on for.

"We have conducted two successful decoy attacks and a boarding raid," Mary continued.

"Master-at-Arms, I want you and the boarding party to practice boarding raids until you can do them in your sleep. I feel we will have need of that tactic in our future skirmishes."

"Yes Ma'am!" Isabel said joyfully.

"I also want you and the boarding party to continue painting your faces. I want those pirate scum to feel absolute terror when they look upon you."

"Who's to be first then?" Anne asked.

"Stede Bonnet."

Mary answered and was greeted with blank faces.

"As they go, he's not your typical pirate. According to what they say about him he's a well to do who desperately wants to play at being a pirate."

This was indeed the case. Sometimes known as the 'Gentleman pirate', not because of his manners but his wealth, Bonnet had had a moderately wealthy upbringing. At some point in his life he had decided that he craved a life of adventure, and the life of a pirate would give him what he desired.

"Where do we find this Bonnet?"

Isabel asked and as she did Mary could hear the lust for the fight in her voice.

"They say he sails the waters around Nassau."

Ms. Jones answered the French woman.

"I should be able to get conformation of this when we return to Port Royal. I have a contact in the Royal Navy who was loyal to my husband."

"Why'r we goin' back to Port Royal?" Anne asked. "If we know he's around Nassau why not go straight there?"

"For starters we have a hold full of dried meat we need to off load."

Mary said in reply to Anne's question.

"Then we need to see Ms. Jones's contact so that we can restock on the chain shot, cannon balls and gunpowder we used against L'Olonnais."

"May I suggest Captain, that as we are here, we off load our cargo in old Panama?" Ms. Jones said.

"It was what we originally intended to do I suppose," Mary

replied. "But let's not get rid of all of it, we may as well provision our own stores."

Later that day the Jenny's Revenge sailed into Panama under a merchant's flag and minimal sails so as not to alarm the locals. When Mary saw the destruction that Morgan and his crew had brought down upon them her heart ached and her temper flared. She wished now that she had driven her Katar through his heart even if he was a Kings man. As they docked the harbour master warily came out to great them and to enquire as to why they had come. As he spoke Mary saw a broken man before her, and then took in the other locals visible in the port. All were scared she could see, that the ship that had just moored could be full of pirates returning to deliver the final blow. Mary, accompanied by Ms. Jones, explained to the harbour master that they had cargo to sell but as the people had lost everything, they could have it. The Boucanee was gratefully received. As well as taking the few valuables that the people had, Morgan's crew had taken most if not all of their food. As they set sail on their return trip to Port Royal, the crew of the Jenny's Revenge were more motivated than ever to return to their vendetta. They all had had their lives destroyed by pirates, and now so had the people of Panama. Mary silently vowed that if Morgan had not danced at the gallows, she would get revenge for Panama.

# Chapter twenty-three.

Women at sea: a figurehead of a woman was common on the masthead of merchant and pirate vessels' alike. Commonly naked as it was thought to calm the seas, her open eyes were believed to serve as a clear guide for safe passage. Yet it was considered bad luck to have an actual woman aboard.

As they dropped anchor in Port Royal, Mary was conscious that one member of her crew could not be seen walking about the streets. After what Rebecca had told her about covering her tracks Mary hoped that if any authorities were interested in the death of Doctor Smith, then they would believe that his assistant was either dead or long gone. Either way Mary didn't want anyone believing otherwise so had ordered Rebecca to stay aboard and below decks for the duration of this visit. Ms. Jones had gone ashore to see if she could get more supplies from her naval contact, whilst Anne in her role as Quartermaster drew up a roster for armed sentries. After their meeting with Morgan Mary had decided that whenever they were in port or at anchor, they would have armed members of the crew on look out. She believed that even if Morgan had gone to the gallows, he may have gotten word out about them. Later that day Ms. Jones returned with news and information that could aid them in their vendetta. Whilst visiting with her contact, he had introduced her to a Benjamin Hornigold. Hornigold had discovered discrepancies in the store that had supplied them with chain shot and had questioned Ms. Jones's contact about it. Unable to come up with a believable explanation he'd ended up giving Hornigold the truth. The truth as it turned out interested Hornigold a great deal. When he had discovered that there was to be a meeting with a member of the pirate hunting crew that he'd just heard about, he had insisted on being there. At their meeting point Ms. Jones was instantly on edge at this stranger's appearance. Even more so when the stranger revealed that he knew the secret of the Jenny's Revenge. Her mind had been put somewhat at ease when this Hornigold had revealed that they were in the same business, the difference being that he worked for Woodes Rodgers, the man sanctioned by the King of Great Briton to end piracy in the Jamaica's.

Hornigold then went on to reveal that he could introduce Ms. Jones's Captain to Rodgers, and if they agreed to certain terms, they would in turn receive targets and supplies. Ms. Jones had agreed to take Hornigold's proposition to her Captain and had been given a time and place to meet.

"Do you trust this Hornigold?" Mary asked her first mate.

"Not entirely, no." Ms. Jones confessed. "But he was vouched for by my contact and when he gave me the location of our meeting it gave him some....levy, shall we say."

Mary raised her eyebrows, curiosity peaked, and Ms. Jones answered her unspoken question.

"We are to meet at the Governor's mansion."

The next evening Mary, Ms. Jones, and Isabel headed for their meeting with Hornigold and the mysterious Woodes Rodgers.The fact that the meeting was in the governor's mansion gave weight to the argument that Hornigold was legit, but all three women believed it could just as easily be a trap. As such they had all chosen to come armed in one way or another. Mary and Ms. Jones had gone for a more subtle approach with their Katars hidden beneath the drape of the long coats they wore. Isabel had gone in completely the other direction. With a bandoleer over each shoulder that put a pistol on each hip and a Katar sheathed on her belt, it was hard not to mistake her for a pirate, especially with her eye patch.

"Ah Ms. Jones, good you came."

Hornigold greeted them at the gates to the mansion grounds.

"And I see you've brought company. May I presume that one of you ladies is the Captain?"

"That would be me," Mary introduced herself.

"Good to meet you Captain Mary..."

133

"Just Mary. We gave up our family names when pirates took everything else from us." Mary explained, her tone bitter.

"I see. And who might this be?"

Hornigold indicated at Isabel who stood glaring daggers at the man before her.

"This is our Master-at-Arms, Isabel."

"Excellent."

Hornigold replied slightly disturbed by the frosty reception the woman was giving him.

"Well if you'll follow me, I have someone to introduce you to who's going to be very important in this area soon."

With that he turned and strode towards the mansion nodding subtly at the shadows either side of the gate. For the first time Mary saw the guards that stood there. She should have known that they would be there and chastised herself for allowing Hornigold to distract her. Once inside the mansion none of the women were surprised to see its abundant opulence. It was typical, Mary thought, of the British Empire. Those of wealth and status lived a life of decadence whilst outside their walls normal people scrabbled in the filth, fighting each other just to eat. As they entered the grand study, two men turned from where they stood by the fireplace to inspect their new comers.

"Ladies, may I introduce our host for this evening, Lieutenant Governor Thomas Lynch."

Although his words and actions acknowledged the man before him as his superior, it wasn't hard to pick up by the tone of his voice that Benjamin Hornigold despised the man he'd just introduced.

Apparently oblivious to Hornigold, Governor Lynch strode forward and offered his hand to Mary. His appearance was not what any of the women expected from an English aristocrat. His clothes were simple and all business, not the pomp and frill many of his stature preferred.

His grey hair was neatly trimmed and his jaw line clean shaved. His facial features also suggested that this was a man who did not laugh a lot.

"Captain Mary."

He said as she took the proffered hand as if to shake it, but neither did. Without turning away she introduced Ms. Jones and Isabel. The whole time she never let her gaze slip from his. She could tell that he was trying to get the measure of the women who stood before him.

"I was led to believe we were supposed to be meeting Woodes Rodgers?" Mary asked and as she did, both she and the Governor decided the hand clasp had gone on long enough.

"That would be you Sir?"

She turned to the man still standing by the fireplace.

"Yes Madam, that would be me."

As he stepped forward to introduce himself, unlike Lynch, he did not offer his hand.

"I am Woodes Rodgers," he announced with authority.

"Should we have heard of you Sir?" Ms. Jones asked.

"Perhaps not," Rodgers replied. "But very soon it will be a name which strikes fear and hatred into those whom you hunt."

The three women looked at the somewhat pompous gentleman before them and then to each other, all silently agreeing that he was having visions of grandeur.

"How do you suppose that will happen?" Isabel asked bluntly, her French accent surprising all the men in the room.

"I have been commissioned by his majesty King George to rid this area of pirates, and he has given me the resources to do so."

Rodgers declared with his chest puffed out. It was as if the very mention of his appointment by the King of Great Briton would be enough to make all bow down before him.

"If I may ask Captain, I couldn't help but notice your crew mate's French accent."
Hornigold said taking the wind out of Rodgers's sails somewhat.
"Do you not all sail under one flag?"
"We do Sir, and that flag would be revenge." Mary replied coldly. "My ship offers sanctuary to all women regardless of race, colour or creed. Sanctuary and the opportunity to destroy those who destroyed them."
"And that is why when Mr. Hornigold mentioned you, I agreed to a meeting."
Rodgers said, once more taking charge of the meeting.
"We are in the same line of business you
and I. We want to rid the world of piracy!"
Mary had to agree that their goals were the indeed the same, and all three women nodded sagely.
"To that end ladies I would like to give you what you need in order to make that happen."
Mary stood dumbfounded at the man's offer.
"I have drafted you a letter that when presented in any of the Kings armouries, they will provision you with whatever you request."
"Thank you Sir!"
Mary said clearly excited by what she had just been told.
That being said suspicion gnawed at the back of her mind.
"What is it you want in return?"
"I see you are no fool madam." Lynch said, his voice coloured with a mild admiration.
"Nothing is for free after all. Whenever you are in Port Royal you will send one of your crew to report to me for assignment. In return I will give you what you need to carry it out."
And there it was Mary thought. They would have what they needed but the price was their liberty.
"I know what you're thinking," Hornigold said.

"But you would be wrong. You will stay independent, but you will be expected to take out the targets we give you."
"Yes ladies," Rodgers took over. "You are also free to carry on with your voyage for revenge."
But his voice suddenly turned bitterly cold.
"Mark my words though ladies. If we should have a conflict of interest or you decide to try and cross me, I shall not hesitate to send you to the bottom of the ocean."

# Chapter twenty-four.

*Cutlass: a short thrusting sword with a flat and slightly curved blade, used in the past especially by sailors and pirates.*

As their meeting came to a conclusion two pieces of information were exchanged between those present. The first was the Jenny's next target. Mary had informed Woodes Rodgers that they intended to hunt down the pirate known as Stede Bonnet. It was agreed between Hornigold and Rodgers that this target would be beneficial to them also. The only difference between Mary's plan and the instructions given to them by Rodgers was that they were not to kill Bonnet. He had to face the judicial system, where upon he would be hanged for piracy. Mary wasn't pleased with the instruction and could tell that the Isabel and Ms. Jones weren't either. But she figured that as long as the world was rid of Bonnet and his crew it didn't matter if they died by her hand or at the end of a rope. The plan was that they were to use their usual tactic of luring their target ship in but they were not to destroy it, merely incapacitate it. Once they had done so, ships under the Royal Navy's command would come in and take Bonnet and his crew into custody. Mary had asked why she and her crew needed to bother if the Navy were going to be just over the horizon. It was Hornigold who had answered her.

"Truth of the matter is, we have tried to bring Bonnet in before but as soon as he sees British ships he turns tail and runs. It is hoped that with your ship taking the lead, we will finally get this pirate."

"How will we know when you have him?" Rodgers asked.

"Simple."

Mary replied with a hint of mischief in her voice.

"We'll set his main sail on fire. That should do the trick."

With the meeting over Hornigold offered to escort them to the gates and bid them a farewell, but as they turned to leave Mary had one final question she had to ask.

"Mr. Hornigold, do you have any news of Captain Henry Morgan?"

Turning back to them with a somewhat puzzled expression

on his craggy features he informed them that Morgan had been arrested upon his return to Port Royal, and as they spoke was on his way back to England and the gallows. The revelation had put a smile upon the lips of all those from the Jenny's Revenge, but only deepened the confusion in Hornigold.

"Why do you ask Captain?"

"Oh no reason."

Mary replied cheerfully.

"Good night Mr. Hornigold, we'll find our own way out."

Upon their return to the Jenny's Revenge every last member of the crew was excited to hear what their Captain had to say.

"Ladies, ladies!"

Mary called out to them indicating for quiet with her hands.

"All in due course, for it is late and I am tired. When we meet for breakfast, I shall tell you all then."

The crew looked more than a little disappointed for as Mary had said, it was late and they had stayed up to hear what had happened.

"Right! You 'eard the Captain!"

Anne bellowed.

"She'll tell you t'morrow. Now those not on watch it's time to pipe down 'n' turn in."

"Thank you Quartermaster."

Mary said with a wry smile.

"With me if you please."

With that she headed for her cabin indicating with an inclination of her head that those who had come back from the mansion were to join her.

"How do you think the crew will take it?" she asked once they were in the privacy of the cabin.

"As we're still carrying out our vendetta, I believe that they will be alright with it."

Ms. Jones answered Mary taking a seat at the Captain's

141

table, where once sat she placed her elbows upon it and steeped her fingers. With no clue as to what had happened, having not been at the meeting, Anne looked around the room before asking,

"So, what 'appened at the mansion then?"

"Woodes Rogers made us a deal. We just have to go after the targets he chooses, when he chooses!"

Isabel grumbled clearly unhappy with their circumstances.

"Is that true Ma'am?"

Anne asked clearly un-eased by the French woman's words.

"Yes. Thank you Isabel."

Mary said, scowling at the Master-at -Arms.

"So, are we still allowed to hunt for ourselves?"

Anne continued with her questions.

"Yes, we're still allowed to choose who we go after."

Mary told her Quartermaster.

"But as Isabel said, we have to go after certain targets of their choosing."

"The upside."

Ms. Jones said, filling Anne in on the deal they had made.

"Is that when we need to restock our inventory, we have a letter signed by Rogers himself saying we can have whatever we need."

"Well, that's good."

Anne said chirpily though her good mood was instantly quashed.

"But if we get in their way or do something they don't like, they send us to see Davy Jones!"

Isabel growled, receiving another angry glare from Mary.

"It was just a threat Anne. As long as we don't get in their way and we hit the targets they give us we'll be fine."

The next morning during breakfast Mary informed the rest of the crew about the deal they had made with Woodes Rodgers. She neglected to tell them about the ultimatum deciding that only her head staff needed to know. The hold burst into a cacophony of questions from the crew at the news.

Do we only take orders from them now?

Are we allowed to go after who we want?

Are we still pirate hunters or are we king's men?

Are we still free or are we slaves to the British?

"QUIET!" Ms. Jones roared. "Let the Captain speak!"

Mary scanned the room trying to figure out who had asked what question but gave up after a few seconds.

"No, we are not king's men or slaves. We are still pirate hunters and we are still free to go after who we want."

She paused after answering all the questions and looked at the crew. Her crew. She made herself stand taller. She was the Captain, she was in command, and it was time to show it.

"The deal that I have made with Rodgers means no more scrabbling about for what we need."

Her voice was strong and confident, and she could tell that she had everyone's attention.

"Our vendetta still stands, we will have our revenge on those who have wronged us. If Rodgers wishes to provide us with some of the names so be it. I assure you it will make no difference to our objective. Believe me ladies when I say that if Rodgers thinks he can get in our way, he'll regret it."

The hold exploded into cheers and Mary knew the crew were still with her.

# Chapter twenty-five.

Greenhorn: somebody who lacks experience and may be naive or gullible.

The following day the Jenny's Revenge sailed with her holds fully laden with provisions and ordinance. After the mornings clear lower deck Mary had ordered that a full inventory be taken so they could see just what the letter Rodgers had given them would get. After presenting it to the stores man at Fort James they had been more than a little surprised to find that they could have everything they had requested. Even more surprising was that they had been given permission to dock in one of the berths reserved for the Royal Navy which had allowed them to store ship quicker and easier. Mary had her reservations about docking as she hadn't wanted anyone to see the crew but when they had arrived at the berth, they found that they were the only ship there so their secret was maintained. To aid with the illusion that they were just an ordinary merchant vessel the women, all except the decoy party, had taken to wearing their hair in the same style as male sailors and strapping their breasts. If anyone had happened to see them loading the ship, they would have seen just another merchant vessel at the docks. To ensure that the Jenny was seen to be a lone merchant vessel they had set sail a full day before the ships of the Royal Navy. They all had some concern about this part of the plan. Yes they were heading in the same direction, and the Navy's ships were undeniably faster than the Jenny, but the feeling remained that they had been sent out not to capture Bonnet but to slow him down and become sacrificial lambs. Mary and the heads of each party had discussed this at great length and had decided that if it looked like the Navy weren't going to show, then they would kill Bonnet and destroy his ship as they had intended to do so in the first place. Now as they sailed the shipping lanes between Nassau and Tortuga, Mary couldn't help but feel excited about being back in the hunt. As she stood on the half deck, she looked about the crew and could tell that they felt the same way.

For too long they had waited but now here they were with a target. The plan for taking Bonnet was a mixture of their decoy tactic along with the boarding technique they had used against Morgan. The decoy party would lure them in as usual, taking out the boarding party. Their own boarders would then swing over and either take the rest of the crew prisoner or kill them. The deal was that as long as Bonnet was able to stand trial, if a few of his crew died in the process, so be it.

"We're coming up on the co-ordinates now Captain." Rose informed Mary from her place at the ship's compass.
"Very good Rose."
Mary replied smiling at her navigator before turning to below orders.
"Drop the mainsail! You know the drill ladies. I want this ship looking like it's adrift!"
Indeed, the crew did know the drill. In a matter of moments the mainsail was down and made to look as though an attempt had been made to raise it. All of the top sails were stowed as if never used and the fore and mizzen sails were made to look as if partly set. All was made to give the illusion that the women on board had tried their best but had ultimately failed. In truth the mainsail was still rigged and could still be easily raised should the need arise that they needed to make a getaway. All the other sails were similarly rigged so well trained were the crew. It was unclear how long they would have to wait before Bonnet's ship, the Revenge, found them if it found them at all. They were well provisioned and could afford to stay in their current state for a few days. All the information they had been given by Rodgers, as well as that from their land crew, had these co-ordinates as the Revenges hunting grounds so it was hoped that they would be discovered with in a day. The other problem they faced was if they were spotted by another merchant vessel, as they would no doubt want to

offer assistance. Yet again it was Anne who had come up with a solution. If they were to be spotted by other merchants, the decoy party were to go below deck to be replaced by the deck hands. They would then make it appear as if they were making to change the mainsail. As luck would have it, no sooner had their preparations been completed, sails were spotted on the horizon.

"Can you tell who it is yet?"

Ms Jones asked the lookout. The reply came down as a negative, but Mary figured that the chances were good that it would be the Revenge.

"Places ladies!"

She ordered and was surprised to see Anne rushing up out of the hold.

"Captain!"

The girl panted clearly in distress.

"It's Lucy. She's sick! Rebecca's with 'er but she don't look right."

"Take me to her."

Mary ordered. This was the last thing she needed at this point in time.

Anne nodded and turned back towards the hold. Not quite walking, not quite running she did an odd kind off skip that if the situation weren't so serious, Mary would have found it amusing. Down in the main hold she was greeted by the sight of the decoy party in various state of undress surrounding Rebecca and Lucy. The head of the decoy party lay on the deck as the ships doctor examined her belly.

"How is she?"

Mary asked, a little more curtly than she intended.

"I think it's food poisoning," Rebecca stated.

" Something she's eaten is disagreeing with her. She'll be fine in a day or two."

"A day or two!" Mary gasped in total disbelief.

"I need her now!"

The decoy party started gabbling between themselves about what they were supposed to do without Lucy, and the noise in the hold became so raucous that Mary couldn't hear Rebecca's reply.

"QUITE!" a voice boomed and for the second time in as many minuets Mary was surprised to see that it was from Anne.

"Thank you Quartermaster," Mary said with a nod. "You were saying Rebecca."

"I said she," and she pointed to Lucy. "Will be good for nothing in her current state. She can barely stand she's so cramped up."

"What the hell are we going to do?"

Mary questioned the universe in general.

"We need someone to take charge of the decoy party."

She said turning to them. The girls of the decoy party just looked to each other shrugging, none of them willing to take the lead position. A cough, which Mary had come to recognise as the birth of an idea, came from behind her.

"Yes Anne?"

Mary said without turning.

"I could take Lucy's place," Anne said sheepishly. "If you like."

Mary whirled on the girl and grabbing her by the shoulders babbled,

"Do you think you can do it?"

"Oh yeah, I pretty much came up with the moves."

She said and the decoy party nodded eagerly in agreement.

"I can do it. But just this once mind, it is Lucy's job after all."

Anne smiled down at the sick woman to show she wasn't trying to take her position away from her. Mary hugged Anne fiercely.

"Get dressed!" she said excitedly.

"We don't have much time."

By the time the decoy party had gotten dressed and on deck, the ship on the horizon had closed the distance between them considerably and more than enough to make out her colours with a spyglass. A black flag with a skull and single horizontal bone could be made out. Many pirates had taken to flying the "Jolly Roger" to signal to other ships who was about to attack them and to surrender or die. Each flag had subtle differences and had been designed by their owners as a way of telling all who they were. This particular design belonged to Stede Bonnet which meant that the Jenny's Revenge had found her target.

"It's him!"

Mary hollered so all on deck could hear, and the message was passed on to those below decks.

"Decoy party, you know what to do. Anne, good luck. I have faith in you."

With that vote of confidence given she ducked down below.

"Right girls!"

Anne said pushing her breasts up and pinching her cheeks to make them rosy.

"You know the drill, now let's get these bastards excited!"

The girls gave each other the once over checking that their corsets were tight and blunderbusses primed and ready. As the Revenge came close enough to see the crew on deck, the decoy party started their act. Cries for help were given and hankies waived. Seeing no perceived threat, the Revenge dropped sails so that they could drift up alongside. Once within shouting distance the question "Who is your Captain?" floated over.

As temporary leader of the decoy party it was Anne who took up the call.

"We 'ave no Captain!"

She replied, voice high pitched and sounding on the edge of

hysteria. "He died of sickness. Many of the crew followed 'im and the rest are bedridden below."

She let out a sob and raised a hand to wipe away invisible tears.

"What caused this sickness?"

A second question came back and this time the two ships were close enough for Anne to be able to see who had asked it. The person with all the questions stood on the main deck and was as well dressed as he was spoken. She knew instantly that she was being addressed by Stede Bonnet, also known as the gentleman pirate.

"I believe that the meat we picked up in our last stop may 'ave been bad."

Anne said creating their latest cover story with every word she spoke. She knew from her experience as a tavern girl that these types of men very rarely listened to what she said, as they were often too busy looking at what she had.

"And how come you lovely ladies don't appear to have suffered?" Bonnet asked and Anne had to agree that it was a reasonable question.

"We 'ad very little of the meat," she replied. "As the men needed it for their strength. So we've suffered very little."

Bonnet seemed satisfied by this, women after all ate far less than men so it seemed only logical that they would suffer less. The two ships were side by side now and although no boarding lines had been thrown, Anne could see that Bonnet's crew were eager to cast them and get over. The decoy party were doing their job well, huddling in two's looking relieved and distressed at the same time whilst all the while exposing just enough flesh to get the pirates blood boiling.

"Do you require any assistance?"

Bonnet asked and no sooner had Anne said that they did, then the boarding line were let loose.

Their hooks glinted in the sun as they flew and then bit into the Jenny's rails as if they too were as hungry for action as the men that threw them. Once the ships were secure the boarding planks rained down giving the men access to the spoils that lay before them.

"Come on men! Let's go help these lovely ladies!"

A voice called out and was greeted with cheers. Anne couldn't help but feel that she recognised that voice and when its owner turned to race over the boarding plank, she saw that it was the baby-faced pirate who had left her to die behind the Cabin boy. As he was about to step up, he to recognised who stood before him.

"You?"

He said plainly confused.

"I thought I'd left you fer dead in that ally. How are you here?"

The rest of Bonnet's crew had stopped in their tracks, intrigue and confusion compelling them to watch what was unfolding before them. Anne said nothing, instead she turned to the nearest member of the decoy party, spun her around and tore the Blunderbuss from the girl corset.

She then leapt to the boarding plank and in two strides was before the baby-faced pirate with the Blunderbuss pointed at his face.

"Hah!" He laughed. "What are you gonna do with that sweet cheeks? Shoo...."

Before he could finish his sentence, Anne had pulled the trigger and turned the man's head to chum. His companions froze where they stood. This was partly due to the sheer level of violence that they had just witnessed and partly because of the overwhelming force they now faced.

The other members of the decoy party had just moved into firing position along with the boarding party who, at the firing of Anne's weapon, had swung down from their hiding place in the rigging to the deck of the Revenge, and now stood with their pistols drawn. Normally a ship's

Captain would remain safely aboard their own ship during boarding operations, but after their encounter with Henry Morgan Mary had decided that she wanted to be in the thick of it all, leading from the front. As such she had been in the rigging and now stood with her boarding party.

"Where is Stede Bonnet?" she growled.

Bonnet's men cleared a path which allowed Mary to stride up to the man and deliver a backhand to his jaw with such ferocity it buckled the man's knees.

"What is the meaning of this?"

Bonnet stammered rubbing his jaw, his eyes watering from the blow.

"You and your crew are pirates Sir, and we intend to see that you are brought to justice."

"What! I'm no pirate!" Bonnet protested. "Just ask my crew."

Mary turned and looked at Stede's crew who were now being closely guarded by her own.

For the most part they just shrugged or shook their heads.

Mary looked down at the sprawled form of Bonnet.

"You are the most pathetic example of a pirate that I have ever seen." She spat.

"Even your own crew have no loyalty or respect for you."

It was true that the crew of the Revenge had no love for their Captain. Stede Bonnet after all was not your conventional pirate. He had not become one the way most had, either by deserting the Navy or falling on hard times. He had become a pirate because he wanted a life of adventure and believed that piracy would give it to him. Stede had actually been a moderately wealthy and well-educated landowner who had inherited his land when his father had died. Not satisfied with this way of life, and possibly because of marital problems, Bonnet had set about becoming a pirate. He'd bought himself a ship and called it the Revenge, even though he sought none. He then hired on a crew who because of his former life had nicknamed him the 'Gentleman pirate'. It soon became clear to the crew that their greenhorn of a Captain had no knowledge of sailing which had led to their complete disrespect for him. Many of them only stayed because unlike most pirate vessels, where coin was earned by splitting the spoils, Bonnet paid his crew.

"Take the crew and lock them in the hold."

Mary ordered. Isabel nodded in acknowledgment then turned to the nearest of Bonnet's crew and stared at him. With her face blackened and eye patch removed her visage resembling that of a skull, no words were needed, the crew knew what was wanted of them. Unarmed and surrounded they had no wish to die, and Isabel's expression made it clear that that was exactly what would happen if they tried anything. Once the deck was clear of the Revenges crew Bonnet continued with his protests about being a pirate, attempting to convince Mary that he'd been forced into it by the crew and even implied that he'd been held a prisoner by Blackbeard himself. A thought visibly passed through his mind before being blurted out.

"I can give you Blackbeard!"

"You can 'give' us Blackbeard."

Mary said, her facial expression and sarcastic tone of voice told all that she was clearly unconvinced.

"And just how are you going to 'give' us Blackbeard?"

"As I said,"

Bonnet replied eagerly, believing he'd just found his ticket to freedom.

"I was prisoner aboard his ship the Queen Anne's revenge. I saw things. Saw people. And pirates! You hunt pirates, yes?"

As he went on, he became more confident in his belief that these women would spare his life for the information that he knew.

He tried to stand but the barrel of Isabel's pistol placed firmly onto his forehead convinced him otherwise.

"You can tell us what you know from down there."

The Master-at-Arms growled.

"If you promise not to kill me, I will tell you everything I know about Blackbeard and his crew."

Thinking he'd just dealt the card that would save his life Bonnet smiled up at Mary. She smiled sweetly back and dealt a card of her own.

"If you tell me all I know then I promise that neither I nor any member of my crew will kill you."

Aware that time was short, as the Royal Navy were possibly only a few hours behind the horizon, Mary decided that the best way to get the man to talk freely was to make him feel comfortable. If he were the 'Gentleman pirate' then she would treat him like a gentleman.

"Please stand up," she said politely.

"Could I get you something to drink?"

Bonnet stood up and after dusting himself off said, "That would be lovely dear lady."

He nodded aft. "There's rum in my quarters."

"I take it none of your crew are in there?"

Mary asked gesturing with her pistol at the cabin door.

"Good god no!"

Bonnet gasped as if the very notion of the idea was simply preposterous.

"Then lead on Sir," Mary told the man before turning to her crew. "Master-at-Arms with me, the rest of you, keep the crew down below. If they try anything; kill them."

Once inside the Captains quarters of the Revenge, Bonnet headed straight to a barrel sitting beside an ornate table. Mary could see that it was full of charts, but Isabel was taking no chances. The Master-at-Arms drew back the hammer on her pistol and the click-click it made sounded like thunder in the otherwise silent cabin. Bonnet froze, his hand midway to a chart.

"Don't try anything."

Mary said almost light heartedly.

"I would hate to have to break a promise."

"It's just a chart! I have no weapons in here." the pirate whimpered.

"Best you don't."

Isabel said coming into Stede's field of view and making it very clear to the man that her pistol was still cocked and pointed at him.

"It's just a chart, I promise you."

As he spoke his head turned rapidly between one woman and the other.

"It has everything you need to know about Blackbeard's future whereabouts."

"And how did you happen to come by this chart exactly?"

Mary asked watching the man closely as he slid it out of its stowage.

"As I said, I was a prisoner of Blackbeard..."

Mary interrupted the man with another question.

"You were a prisoner and yet privy to your captors' charts?"

She raised an eyebrow to show what she thought of Bonnet's words.

"Believe what you will Madam. Do you want to know what I do or not?" Bonnet's tone indicated that if she wasn't careful, promise or not, he wouldn't be revealing anything.

Not wanting to lose such an opportunity Mary returned to the tactic of boosting the man's ego.

"I apologise Sir for my flippancy."

She said bowing her head slightly as if in supplication.

"Please do go on."

The gesture seemed to appease the pirate and he unrolled the chart onto the table.

"Each of these marks are where Blackbeard believes that he will be able to conduct raids upon the Spanish ships returning from the America's." Bonnet paused in his dialog to roll up the chart and present it to Mary as if it were the Holy Grail.

"Take it dear lady, in exchange for my life."

Mary took the offered chart bowing as she did so.

"Thank you Sir. Now tell me, what do you know of his crew?"

Bonnets expression told the two women that he'd more than held up his end of the bargain but after glancing at the intensity of Isabel's cyclopic stare, he relented to sharing more of the information he had about the world's most notorious pirate.

"The crew of the Queen Anne's revenge are about as despicable a bunch of pirates as there ever was or will be. That being said they fear and respect their Captain. He keeps a tight rein on them, and they do as he orders without argument."

He paused, rubbing at his chin as he stared off into the distance obviously trying to remember something.

"There is one amongst his crew one that you definitely want to steer clear of."

Bonnet continued, but in a hushed voice as if just speaking the man's name aloud would seal his death warrant.

"Black Caesar. Even Blackbeard himself has trouble controlling that one."

A shout of sails on the horizon brought an end to their meeting. All three stepped back onto the upper deck.

"Can you make out who it is?"

Isabel questioned the boarding party. After a short back and forth of information with the lookout aboard the Jenny, it transpired that three ships could be seen all flying British colours. Mary turned to the boarding party and ordered them to slip one of the Revenges Perry boats and set it

157

alight.

"That should be enough of a signal," she said smiling as she did.

"What do you mean signal?" Bonnet raged. "We had an accord!"

"And we still do Sir." Mary said earnestly. "I promised that I wouldn't kill you and I haven't."

Bonnet's composure snapped.

"You bitch!"

He shrieked and charged Mary, hands outstretched for her throat. Before he'd made it two steps the but of Isabel's pistol smashed into the back of his head sending the man's unconscious body to the deck.

"Thank you Master-at-Arms."

Mary said nodding her thanks to Isabel. She turned to the boarding party and ordered,

"Ladies, if you'd be so kind as put the Captain here with the rest of his crew."

As the women opened the hatch to the main hold to carry out their Captains orders, they revealed that the crew of the Revenge had been busy below decks. Two of the ship's cannons were being moved into a firing position having been obviously primed during their Captains betrayal of information.

"Ah, ah, ah, gentlemen."

Isabel admonished waggling a finger mockingly.

"I would not do that if I were you. If you open your larboard ports you will see our guns are already pointing at you."

It was true. During the planning of this raid, all of the Jenny's command staff had agreed that their guns were to be primed and ready to fire. If the pirates had not surrendered as they had, the gun crew were to send them to the bottom of the ocean regardless of their orders from Woodes Rodgers.

# Chapter twenty-six.

The heads: area at the bow of the ship where sailors relieved themselves. Accompanied with a tow rag which was towed in the water and dragged up in order to clean ones behind before being placed back in the water to get clean.

The smoke from the blazing Perry boat did as Mary had hoped and It wasn't long before the sails of the Naval vessels could be seen cresting the horizon. From time to time whilst they waited, Mary had the boarding party lift the hatch to the Revenge's cargo hold to make sure Bonnet and his men were behaving themselves. It was a task that was becoming more and more unbearable as time went on. As they had been locked up below decks for hours, the crew of the Revenge had taken to relieving themselves in the corner of the hold. Their attempt at keeping the mess to one area was admirable, but with the lack of airflow the stench had quickly built up. Mary and Ms. Jones had used the time to investigate the Captains quarters further. They had found a few charts, which although showed nothing special, they were for waters which they themselves didn't hold. One of them was for around the tip of Florida and seemed to concentrate on a small group of islands. There were a number of areas where a ship could sail but without the chart it looked as if running aground was a real possibility. Mary was studying the chart and had noticed one island in particular had been marked with a cross, when Ms. Jones called for her to come and look at something she had found.

"What do you think it could be?"

She asked when Mary came over, rolling up the charts she had just been studying before tucking them up under her armpit, before Ms. Jones presented her with a ball made of fired clay. It filled her hand and when she inspected it, she found it had a hole in the top and appeared to be hollow. After holding it to her ear and giving it a shake, and then close to her eye to peer inside, she looked at Ms. Jones and shrugged.

"Where did you find it?" she asked.

"There's a case of them under his bed"

Ms. Jones replied still looking at the object with perplexed curiosity. Mary handed the charts she had been holding to her and then knelt beside the bunk and pulled the case in question out. There were perhaps twenty of the odd little balls. She inspected a few of the others but was still none the wiser.

"We'll take them over to the Jenny." She told Ms. Jones. "After all, if they were important enough that Bonnet wanted to keep them hidden then I think we should have them."

Ms. Jones nodded her agreement and then suggested that their friends in the Navy might know what they were.

"An excellent idea."

Mary agreed with her first mate. She scooped a few of them from the case.

"But we'll tell them that these are the only ones we found."

Ms. Jones smiled in understanding.

"In case they decide to confiscate them."

Mary nodded, pleased that they were both thinking along the same lines. Their rummaging completed the two women returned to the upper deck to find the naval vessels were a little over a mile away. Mary ordered Ms. Jones to quickly return to the Jenny and hide their findings whilst she prepared to meet with the Navy. The crew of the Jenny's Revenge were surprised to see that the Navy's boarding techniques were rather similar to those carried out by pirates, and Mary absently mindedly wondered who had taught whom. As soon as they were secured alongside, the Navy's boarding party came over and once satisfied that it was safe to do so, signaled back to their own ship that the rest could come over. The next to come aboard was most definitely an officer judging by his uniform.

Mary also presumed that he was the Captain and as soon as his feet were firmly on the deck she moved to introduce herself, but the man before her beat her to it.

"I am Colonel William Rhett of the Royal Naval vessel Henry, and you are?"

"Captain Mary of the Jenny's Revenge."

She answered mimicking the man's introduction.

"My crew and I have captured the pirate Stede Bonnet and his crew."

Rhett's expression indicated that he was mildly surprised at the woman's words. He was even more surprised when she told him that, as per the orders of Woodes Rogers, Bonnet was alive.

"I can't promise as to what shape he may be in." she continued.

"After confessing his innocence, and that the crew had made him do it, we put him down in the hold with them."

Rhett smiled at the news.

"I'm sure he's been given nothing more than what he deserves."

"He deserves to die," Mary said coldly. "And if it wasn't for Rogers orders I would have seen to it myself."

Rhett nodded solemnly. He himself had been a victim of piracy which, unbeknown to Mary and her crew, was the reason that he now worked for the Navy.

"I assure you Captain; Bonnet and his crew will be brought to justice. Now if that is all I'll let you be on your way."

Presuming that their meeting was adjourned, Rhett turned to leave only to discover that Mary wasn't quite finished.

"One more thing Major."

She said and pulled the odd balls they had discovered from her coat pocket.

"Have you ever seen these before?"

She handed them over to Rhett for his inspection.

"We found them in the Captain's cabin."

Rhett gave them a quick once over before handing them back.

"They're called Grenadoes or powder flasks."

He answered and at Mary's blank expression explained their purpose. "You put a length of slow burning match in the hole and then fill them with gunpowder. Light the match and then throw at your enemies. When they go off, do not get in their way."

With that he tipped his hat and returned to his ship. Pleased with their new find Mary and her boarding party returned to the Jenny where she ordered all lines be cut and sails raised. As they sailed away Mary looked back to the Revenge and the Henry. Rhett struck her as a man of his word and she was confident that Bonnet would soon be dead.

# Chapter twenty-seven.

*Perry boat: Rowboat stored on the upper decks of larger sailing ships for the purpose of going ashore whilst at anchor.*

The following day Mary gathered Ms. Jones, Anne, Isabel and the boarding party on the main deck of the Jenny's Revenge to explain what the odd little balls were that they had discovered in Bonnet's cabin. She told them how they were actually for throwing at your enemy, repeating what Rhett had told her the day before. Isabel was then sent to get a cask of gunpowder and a length of slow match so they could test one.

"How long does the slow match need to be?"

Isabel asked as she slid it into the hole in the Grenadoe.

"Rhett never said."

Mary confessed wishing that she had pestered the man for more information.

"He did say that you don't want to be around one when it goes off though."

Isabel thought about that and then Cut the match to what she thought was an appropriate length. Then she primed the ball with the gunpowder, but when she had filled it to the brim looked at Mary with a puzzled expression.

"What's the matter?"

Ms. Jones asked coming over to take a closer look.

"What will stop the powder simply falling out when you throw it?"

Isabel asked and all agreed that it was a good question.

"Bit of candle wax or deck tar would solve that problem."

Anne said casually whilst looking over Ms. Jones's shoulder.

"Excellent idea!"

Mary said excitedly and a member of the boarding party was dispatched to her cabin to get a candle. She quickly returned and gave Isabel the stump of a burned-out candle. Isabel thanked her and then cut of a chunk of wax, softened it between her fingers, and then stuffed it into the hole in the Grenadoe sealing the gunpowder inside.

She then presented it primed and ready to Mary, who

received the explosive gratefully but then looked around the ship in confusion.

"What's the matter?" Anne asked her.

"Well, how do we test it?" Mary replied still looking for somewhere to throw their latest weapon.

"We could always float it I suppose," Ms. Jones mused. "If we put it in a little crate or the likes."

Anne suddenly ran off below decks and returned a few moments later with a crate from the galley.

"'ere you go." She said handing it to Isabel. "That should do the trick."

They were all excited at the prospect of seeing the Grenadoe explode. One of Perry boats was quickly lowered, and Isabel climbed down into it. As she had explained, as the Master-at-Arms it should be her that lit the fuse, and no one was inclined to disagree with her. Once in the boat Isabel set about lighting the slow match with her tinder box. As soon as the match was alight, she had it in the crate and set it adrift. All those on the upper deck had stopped what they were doing and had gathered to watch. As the crate floated away the anticipation of the moment built; but after two or three minutes of waiting, nothing had happened.

"Maybe the match went out?" Anne said straining her eyes to see if that were the case.

All of a sudden there was a shrill 'BOOM!' and the crate that the Grenadoe had been sat in was turned to kindling and the area around it was peppered with shrapnel. A few of the on lookers jumped in surprise but most cheered at the fire pots crescendo. Ms. Jones turned to Mary, a look of delight on her face.

"I think perhaps a shorter match in future."

Mary nodded her agreement and clapped her first mate on the back.

"Not too short though," she said. "I'd hate for one of those things to go off in your hand."

# Chapter twenty-eight.

Slow match: a match or fuse that burns without a flame very slowly or at a known rate and is used to set off explosives.

*U*pon their return to Port Royal, Mary set about finding as much information about Blackbeard as possible. Her land crew were all given orders to ask discrete questions as they served drinks and bodies to their patrons. Each evening Mary would venture out to meet with one of them to see what they had learned. It took around a week and come the end of it, Mary had discovered more than she had ever imagined. Whilst Mary busied herself with the land crew, Ms. Jones visited the Governor's mansion to see if there were any orders for them. As it turned out there weren't, but they were congratulated on a job well done. The mansion itself was extremely busy. There was to be a new Governor, a John Vaughn, and he was bringing a new deputy with him. From the mansion Ms. Jones went to the storehouses with their latest requests. During their return voyage it had been decided that they needed a new cannon, a ship killer. Although the cannons on the Jenny were powerful enough, they were the ones that she already held when Mary had liberated the ship from the pirate Ned Low. Normally the guns on a pirate ship were smaller with the intension of disabling their opponents. They had been lucky so far that the two ships they had used their guns on were both sloops and quite small. The Jenny had also unleashed all her guns at once in a surprise attack that had destroyed both vessels instantly. The attacks on both Morgan and Bonnet hadn't needed the guns but it was agreed that on the bigger ships, even with the element of surprise, the destruction might not be enough to swing the odds in their favor. So something bigger was required. It was hoped that the letter provided by Woodes Rogers would secure them one of the fortress guns. One of those would be capable of taking out even a capital ship. She met with the store man and made their demand. He simply looked at her and started laughing.

"I have a letter from Woodes Rogers himself that says we can have whatever we need."

"You might well have a letter from Rogers." The store man said.

"But you aint getting one of them fort guns."

He folded his arms and drew himself up as tall as he could, trying to intimidate Ms. Jones with his size. She found his attempt quite amusing after some of the things they had seen.

"If not one of the fort guns do you have anything that heavy we can have?"

Slightly annoyed that she hadn't been put off by his stance when many in the fort had, He sighed and said,

"Come with me."

He turned and started towards the main store house.

"We have some old ships Demi-cannons back here."

He explained as he walked.

"They're thirty-two pounders so should sink anything you point them at."

"So why don't you use them anymore?"

Ms. Jones asked truly puzzled if they were that effective.

"Well, they're not very accurate," the store man confessed.

"You pretty much have to be right beside your target to have any chance of hitting it."

That information put a smile on Ms. Jones's lips. The Demi-cannons would be perfect for their needs. The smile quickly vanished though when she actually saw the Demi-cannons. There were eight of them in total and judging by the state of them they had been sitting behind the store for a number of years. After a quick inspection it turned out that of the eight only two were in a usable condition, and they still needed some work before they could be fired.

"Could I take the both of them?"

Ms. Jones asked the store man. For his part the store man simply shrugged and nodded his head.

"I don't think anyone will miss these love." He answered her.

"So they're all yours."

Ms. Jones thanked the man and after making the arraignments for their pickup, departed to return to the Jenny. As she made to leave through the gates, she discovered that the guards had changed since she had entered when they challenged the strange woman who was walking freely around their fort.

"HALT!"

One of the pair ordered. He lowered his musket so that it was pointing at Ms. Jones and walked towards her.

"Identify yourself and state your business here."

The guard was young and obviously new to the service.

"I'm here on official business at the invitation of Benjamin Hornigold." Ms. Jones answered in as official a tone of voice as she could muster.

"There's no Hornigold here miss," the second guard said placing a hand on the shoulder of the first to calm him.

"He sailed for New Spain last week on official business."

Unperturbed the first guard shrugged off his companion's hand and continued with his questioning.

"If you work for Mister Hornigold, I take it you have proof of what you say?"

"I have a letter from Woodes Rodgers within my coat. If I may?"

Ms. Jones answered and at a nod from the second guard carefully removed the letter from Woodes Rogers from inside her coat and handed it to him whilst the first kept his weapon trained on her.

"It's authentic," the second guard said after inspecting the letter.

"It has a signature and seal from Woodes Rodgers on it."

Reluctantly the first guard lowered his musket.

"Be on your way then."

He said sulkily, unable to hide his disappointment that he hadn't just captured an infiltrator. When she arrived back at the Jenny's Revenge, Ms. Jones found an anxious and irritable Mary pacing the upper deck.

"Where the hell have you been?" Mary snapped when Ms. Jones came aboard.

"I've been up at the fort Ma'am, securing us two heavy canons."

This drew Mary up short, and she looked at Ms. Jones as if she had said something unexpected.

"Sorry?" She said with confusion.

"Did you say two canons?"

Ms. Jones went on to explained how they had come to be the owners of two smaller guns than the one she had been sent out for. She also told how she had been delayed by the two guards on her return due to Hornigold's absence from the island.

"Good." Mary said firmly.

"We're going to need those guns when we go after Hornigold."

"What!"

Ms. Jones spluttered, stunned by what her Captain had just told her.

"Why are we going after Hornigold?" She asked in disbelief.

"I thought we shared the same goal?"

"We do, now."

Mary agreed and then went on to tell her first mate all she had learned from one of the members of the land crew.

Most of them had told her variations of the same tale when it came to Blackbeard. His real name was Edward Teach or Thatch. His reputation was that of being one of the most feared men on the high seas by both his victims, and his own men. Those who had survived an encounter with Blackbeard described him as being a hulk of a man, and when raiding ships he would put slow matches under his hat which would enshroud his head in a halo of smoke and fire. With his wild eyes and thick black beard, many had said that he looked like the devil himself. It had even been rumored one night whilst drinking with some of his crew in his cabin, he had killed one of them. The story went that Blackbeard had drawn two of his pistols and after plunging the room into darkness, fired them. When the candles were re-lit two of his crew lay on the deck. One dead the other screaming having taken a shot to the knee. When asked why he had done it, Blackbeard answered darkly,

"So none of you forget who I am."

It was the last member of the land crew however who had revealed one very important piece of information that none of the others had. Who Blackbeard had learned his trade from. One Benjamin Hornigold. It turned out that before he had turned to hunting them, Hornigold had been one of the most successful pirates in the Bahamas. He had helped to establish the 'Republic of pirates' in Nassau and it was during this time that he had taken on a young Teach as his apprentice. It was only after he had been betrayed by his own men that Hornigold had taken the Kings pardon and had started working for Woodes Rodgers, using his knowledge to hunt down his former brethren.

"So he lied to us!" Mary said seething with rage.

"He's as guilty as any he would send us after. He only wants revenge for the betrayal he feels he has suffered. If not for that betrayal he would still be one of them!"

Ms. Jones visibly shook with anger, but it was with herself that was angry. That she had been taken in by this charlatan from the very beginning. It was clear to her now that Hornigold was only using the Jenny's Revenge to exact his vengeance on those who had cheated him.

"I know where he is." she told Mary her voice strained and low.

"They told me at the fort that he sailed for New Spain last week."

"Then we know where our heading is." Mary replied.

# Chapter twenty-nine.

The Kings pardon: Between the years 1717 to 1718 in an attempt to end piracy in the West Indies, king George the first granted a pardon to those pirates willing to surrender to any colonial governor of the British empire giving them a clean slate.

Even though they were the best of the bunch, the two Demi-cannons still required quite a bit of work before they would be able to fire. The gun crews would also need to practice with the new guns. Unlike the one's already aboard the Jenny which were loaded in the conventional way of down the length of the barrel, the Demi-cannons were breach loaded. This meant a section at the back of the cannon needed to be removed to load it. It allowed for faster reloads as the cannon didn't need to be pulled all the way back into the ship. To accommodate the larger weapons the Jenny would also need to be worked on. The thirty-six pounders were much larger and heavier than the twenty pounders they had, so the deck needed re-enforcing and the gun ports enlarging. These modifications would have to be done at sea as if they were to stand a chance of intercepting Hornigold, it would have to be on his return journey. He had embarked upon his voyage over a week before the Jenny had set sail and it was hoped that they would find the former pirate within a week of setting sail themselves. That should give them the time they needed to carry out the work needed, and train with the new guns. This was also going to be the first traditional sea battle that the Jenny's Revenge and her crew had faced. Mary was planning that they would be able to hit Hornigold with a surprise attack as he wouldn't be expecting to take fire from an ally. The trade routes between New Spain and the Caribbean were well travelled, and Mary intended to use that to her advantage as well. With the modifications to the gun deck and ports completed, the crew were practicing with reloading techniques when sails were spotted on the horizon. The wind had started to get up, so Ms. Jones had the crew drop down the sails to just the main. It was, according to the charts they had, an area fraught with reefs and they didn't want to find themselves accidentally getting blown onto one. They came onto the same heading and waited to see who they shared the waves with. As the ship was under full sails, it didn't take long for them to start to draw level with the Jenny and as it came to within three cables the ship started to drop sails so as to match speeds. On the deck stood Benjamin Hornigold with a look of confusion painted on his face. Unbeknown to Mary and her crew, he had only dropped his sails because he recognised the Jenny's Revenge on the same course that they themselves were on. As they were now level he called out to the crew on deck, curious as to why Captain Mary and her crew out here. Although the sea had picked up in the wind, Hornigold's helmsman was skilled enough that he was able to keep the two ships within hollering distance.

"Ahoy!" Hornigold called over. "Captain Mary!"

Mary, already deck, acknowledged the man's hail by walking to the rails of the Jenny.

"What brings you to these waters?" Hornigold questioned. As far as he knew there were no pirates who preyed in these waters, and he knew full well that she had no orders to be out here from Rogers.

"I'm here for you Captain Hornigold!"

Mary stated in answer to the man's question.

"You've been sent out to escort us?" He questioned the other Captain.

He presumed that as he had been to New Spain on official business for Woodes Rogers that the man had sent the Jenny's Revenge to escort him back to New Providence.

"We need no escort dear lady. Go about your business."

"You miss understand me."

Mary said her anger growing by the second at the man.

"We have come for you and you alone."

"I don't think I understand you madam?"

Hornigold answered now more confused than ever.

What did she mean that they had come for him alone?

"You lied to us!"

Mary roared no longer to contain her anger.

"You are nothing more than a pirate!"

"Not anymore," he retorted. "I put that life behind me."

"Only because you were betrayed by your men. If they hadn't turned against you, you would still be one of them!" she raged.

When the man had no more answers for her, in Mary's mind he had just confirmed her words as true.

"Your crew are no doubt innocent of piracy."

Mary continued and then issued an ultimatum.

"I will give you this one chance to surrender, for their sake, or they will suffer the same fate as you."

In answer to Mary's demands Hornigold grabbed the wheel of his ship, barging his helmsman to the deck as he did so. His intention was clear, that he intended to ram the Jenny. The move was sudden and supposed to take them by surprise, and had the seas been calm it would have worked. But the sea was not calm and as such Amy had plenty of time to evade the maneuver.

"Ready cannons!"

Came a cry from Hornigold's ship, but the Jenny already had hers in position. So when the order came to fire from Hornigold, the Jenny at the orders of Ms. Jones, had already let loose a volley from half her guns. The sea state was both for and against them. Their own shots went high with one of them just clipping the top of Hornigold's foremast. As for Hornigold's shots, the lack of preparation for aiming mixed with the roll of the ship caused their shots to fall short. First volley away and seeing that Captain Mary and her crew were serious about killing him, Hornigold veered away from the Jenny's Revenge.

He hoped to put some distance between them that would allow his gun crews time to reload and get their eye in. He ordered for more sails and quickly put the breathing space he wanted between them. Ms. Jones saw what he was

180

attempting to do and ordered for one of the Demi-cannons to be fired. The thirty-two pounder let loose with a roar like an angry beast. The stores master had been correct when he had said that they were not accurate guns over distance, and once more their shots soared over Hornigold's ship. If she were a betting woman though, Ms. Jones thought, she reckoned that anybody stood on the deck of Hornigold's ship would have soiled themselves when that shot flew over. Seeing this for herself Mary bellowed orders over the growing winds.

"Keep those Demi-cannons firing!" She cried.

She was Pointing ahead of Hornigold's ship, which had veered even further away from them.

"I don't want them to have time to think. We don't need to hit them, just keep driving them forward!"

Ms. Jones looked at her quizzically and then to where she was pointing. There in the distance was what looked to be an island.

"You're going to try and run them aground?" She asked doubtfully.

"Remember the charts Ms. Jones," Mary told her.

"This whole area is littered with reefs. With us hounding them, and a little luck, they'll run right into one."

Ms. Jones looked at Hornigold's ship and the sails she was carrying.

"At their speed and with this wind they'll tear their hull out from under them if they hit!"

"Exactly Ms. Jones! Exactly!"

Their conversation was abruptly ended when the port rail amidships exploded into a cloud of splinters when it was hit by a shot from their prey.

Two of the upper deck crew were caught in the maelstrom.

"Rebecca!" Ms. Jones screamed.

She directed the girl to the two casualties as the Barber-surgeon arrived on deck.

At the same time Mary hollered for Isabel.

"Master-at-Arms!"

When the French woman stuck her head out of the hatch Mary strode over to her, clapped one hand on her shoulder and pointed to Hornigold's ship with the other.

"Fire all cannons! If their guns can reach us, ours can reach them!"

Mary then returned her attention to the two downed crewmen.

"How are they?" she asked Rebecca.

The Barber-surgeon looked up from where she attended the injuries of one of the women. Her arms were soaked in blood as she applied dressings to the woman's face and chest.

"Sorry Captain, there's nothing I can do for that one."

She looked over to where the still body of the second woman lay where she'd fallen.

"She took a splinter to the throat. By the time I got up on deck she'd already bled out."

"What of this one?"

Mary asked kneeling beside the injured woman. She felt sick to her core that these two had shed blood for the Jenny and she couldn't even remember their names.

"She'll live," Rebecca told her.

"But as soon as I've finished she needs to go below."

Mary nodded and stroked the woman's hair and offering a weak smile of reassurance. The roar from the Demi-cannons quickly brought her back to the moment. She rose to her feet and returned to her position beside Amy at the helm.

"Keep bringing us into that pirate," she told the girl.

"If we can't force them onto a reef, then we'll run them to ground on that island."

Amy nodded her understanding of the order. Next Mary barked orders to her First mate.

"Give me more sails Ms. Jones! We need to keep level with that ship."
"But Captain! The winds are almost hurricane!"
Ms. Jones protested, shouting so as to be heard.
"Between that and the seas...."
Mary cut her off mid-sentence.
"I understand your concerns." She told her.
"But if we're to give our guns a chance we have to stay level!"
Ms. Jones nodded reluctantly and then ordered for the sprit and lower fore sails to be raised. She hoped that as they were smaller and lower down they wouldn't unbalance the Jenny in the tumultuous seas. The two extra sails accelerated the Jenny, allowing her to draw up on Hornigold's ship. This allowed their next volley of shots to be fully broadside, even though they were separated by two hundred fathoms. Again high seas thwarted them and most of their shots failed to find their marks, but one from a Demi-cannon did hit just forward of midships. The damage it caused wasn't significant, but it did cause Hornigold to put even more distance between them. Unfortunately, another one of Hornigold's shots was also successful. The Jenny was hit on her bow, and although the shot did not punch all the way through, it did severely crack the hull dangerously close to the waterline.
"Get hot pitch into those cracks!" Anne shouted at the spare hands.
The cracks had already started to let water into the hold and in these seas it would only be a matter of time before the hull boards failed. Anne knew they had little time to seal and shaw the damage. In her haste, one of the spare hands lost her footing and with the rolling deck stumbled heavily splashing hot pitch from the bucket she was carrying over her crewmate who was waiting to help with the repairs. The pitch slopped onto the woman's leg setting her britches

alight. Rebecca having returned from the upper deck witnessed the whole affair and was the first to react. She grabbed one of the buckets of sand placed around the decks in case of fires and threw it on the woman's burning breaches.

"Margret!"

The girl who had been carrying the pitch shrieked.

"Margret! I'm so sorry!"

She went to kneel beside her fallen crewmate, but Anne grabbed the girl buy the shoulders, stared her right in the eye and in her sternest voice said,

"There'll be time for sorry later. If you don' get pitch on them cracks we'll all be done for!"

Taken aback by the sternness of Anne's voice the girl nodded vigorously and went straight to her task.

Anne turned back to Rebecca and found her slicing Margret's breaches open on her burned leg. Margret for her part was laying on her side trying to stay as still as possible so that Rebecca could do her job. The pitch had burned through the woman's breaches into her skin and was in fact still burning its way into her leg. Rebecca looked up at Anne and demanded water. Anne understood, grabbed the sand bucket and used it to scoop up the water that had seeped through the cracked hull. She poured the water onto the burning pitch on Margret's leg cooling it down. As it cooled the pitch hardened, allowing Rebecca to begin pick it out with the tip of her knife. Margret screamed and sat bolt upright.

"Hold her down!"

Rebecca ordered Anne, and then reached into the bag that she had taken to carrying around everywhere she went. From it she pulled two items, a folded strip of leather and a small bottle of rum. The strip of leather she gave to Margret and told her to bite down on it. Then she poured the rum onto the burns. Margret screamed and bit down. Anne held her firmly but kept her eye on the repairs at the same time. By the time Rebecca had finished, Margret was sobbing in Anne's arms but the Quartermaster knew that there was no time for sympathy. As kindly as she could she told Margret to find somewhere safe and returned her attention back to patching up the Jenny. Back up on deck the weather had moved from becoming, to being a hurricane. It now took both Amy and Mary to hold the ship steady and the wind was threatening to tear what few sails they had raised from their masts. On Hornigold's ship it looked like they were fairing far worse. They were still running full sails but from what Mary could see it looked as if they had tried to reduce sails. One of the top sails was flapping relentlessly where it had gotten loose while they were trying to take it down. They had also stopped firing on the Jenny which meant Mary had one less thing to worry about. As for themselves they continued to fire on Hornigold, timing their shots so that they still pushed him towards the island and reefs. And then it happened. Hornigold's ship seemed to come to an abrupt stop, dead in the water. As the swell they were on dropped down, it revealed the reef it was hiding and threw Hornigold's ship onto it tearing out the hull. Although their movement had been initially arrested by the reef, with full sails on their masts, the ship was then dragged over it and on its side. Bodies were thrown overboard to drown or to be smashed and torn on the reef. Satisfied that in these conditions and with the damage they had sustained, Hornigold and his crew were done for, Mary called for the gunners to cease fire. She then realised that if they kept their current course then they too would suffer the same fate. She and Amy wrestled the wheel and pointed the Jenny out into deeper waters.

# Chapter thirty.

Cannons: a weapon that fired heavy iron balls or other projectiles through a simple iron tube. The primary weapon on sail ships during the golden age of piracy.

The Jenny's Revenge sailed into Port Royal gingerly under minimum sails. They had weathered the hurricane, but it had not been the most comfortable of nights. They managed to drop all sails so as not to break a mast but one of the deck crew, an older woman by the name of Agnes, had broken her arm in the process. Their intention now was to take some time and carry out the repairs needed on the Jenny. The relentless pounding they had delivered to Hornigold had seriously depleted them of gunpowder and cannon balls, and Mary hoped that their letter from Woodes Rogers would still hold good so they could replenish their stocks. Mary knew that there was no way that anybody could find out about them taking out Hornigold, but you could never tell though if the latest political standpoint had changed from one visit to the next, rendering their letter useless. Ms. Jones had informed her that upon her last visit to the mansion they had been preparing for the arrival of a new Governor. This latest man, whoever he might be, might decide that he no longer had to honor any previous arraignments regardless of where they came from. As usual it was Ms. Jones who went to the Governor's mansion to see if Rogers had left them any orders. She would then seek out her contact in the fort store house for it was felt that if the letter no longer held sway, at least they might be able to replenish some of their supplies. On her way to the mansion Ms. Jones passed by the main town square and could see that some new gallows were being erected. They were larger than usual, with room for more than one person, and she made a mental note to ask who was going to be dancing from them. Mary in the meantime would be visiting the land crew. She intended to see if she could put those who had been injured somewhere safe to recover, and perhaps gain a few new members for the Jenny to take their place. She also hoped to get some more information about Blackbeard and his crew. Her earlier enquiries had been dropped when she had learned about Hornigold, but she now intended to resume the hunt. In the taverns and brothels though, there was no other subject on the lips of the patrons other than that of the hangings. By simply sitting and listening to those around her Mary discovered that there was to be a multiple pirate hanging. The pirates in question were the notorious Jack Rackham, aka Calico Jack, and his cohorts Anne Bonny and Mary Read. They were to face trial and if found guilty, which they most surely would be, they would take a long drop with a short rope. It was common for pirates to be hung in public so as to make an example of them. The hanging of a female pirate though, let alone two of them, was unheard of and was sure to bring in the crowds. The situation reminded Mary of their own predicament and she hated to think what would happen to any of them if they should be caught by pirates. The thought made her shudder involuntarily and she vowed that it would never happen. The proprietor of the tavern in which Mary presently sat snapped Mary out of her musings. He and his wife were sympathetic to her cause, having moved from England in hopes of a better life, only to find their clientele were mostly piratical and threatened their lives most every day. He agreed that he could take on two more staff and Mary thanked him expressing that it would only be until they were well again. She turned to Margret and Agnes and told them to take care but to keep their eyes and ears open for anything they might find useful. Upon her arrival at the Governor's mansion Ms. Jones found herself being invited into the grounds and being escorted, with a good many people from the port to a large room in the house that had been converted into a courthouse. After being shown to a seat Ms. Jones was told by those around her that she was to be privy to the trial of Calico Jack and the two women pirates Anne Bonny and Mary Read. All of those present were to be witness' to ensure that justice was being upheld. All of them were extremely excited at the prospect of seeing the trial of the woman pirates, so much so that Calico Jack had almost become an afterthought. The three defendants were led into the courtroom in shackles. The trial went as expected, pirate trials were for the most part just for show with a forgone conclusion. Jack appeared to be resigned to his fate, but the two women had other ideas. When asked if they had anything to say both pleaded with their bellies. This drew gasps of shock and outrage from many of the trials onlookers which surprised Ms. Jones. After all, if these women were willing to cavort with pirates why should it be so shocking that they would be pregnant out of wedlock. The Lieutenant Governor, John Vaughan, who was presiding over the procedures called for silence, and after a moment the noise in the room died down. He then passed judgement over the three stood before him.

"You have all been accused of and found guilty of piracy. Therefore you will all hang from the neck until you are dead."

He paused to allow his words to sink in.

"In the case of you ladies, as you are quick with child, you will have a stay of execution until your innocent unborn infants are delivered. You will stay in incarceration until that time and then you will be shown to the gallows."

Sentences passed the three pirates were taken from the courtroom by the Governors men into the back of an open cart. The Lieutenant Governor was the last to exit and addressed the pirates once more.

"John Rackham, you will face the gallows immediately and your crew will bear witness."

Rackham let out an involuntary sob which drew glares of contempt from Bonny and Read.

The cart left the Governors grounds but did not go immediately to the gallows. Instead, the three condemned were paraded through the streets of Port Royal as a warning to others who still practiced piracy. Many from the trial chose to follow the procession, but Ms. Jones decided to go straight to the town square. She had decided that there was no point trying to see if there were any orders for them. In light of the day's events, she would just have to return another day. At the town square she was surprised to find Mary in the small but growing crowd. Ms. Jones informed her Captain about the happenings at the Governor's mansion and was amazed to find that Mary knew exactly what was going on. She had discovered by talking with various people in the taverns she'd been to exactly who the three pirates were. Ms. Jones on the other hand knew very little about the three whose trial she had just attended so Mary told her all that she had learned. Jack Rackham and Anne Bonny had met and fallen in love when she was a barmaid in the tavern he frequented in Nassau. The problem was that Anne was married and try as they might, they couldn't get her husband to let her go. In desperation Jack offered to buy Bonny from her husband but when even that failed, they simply fled. They commandeered a sloop and before long started conducting pirate raids on merchant ships.

"She's just like me!" Mary told Ms. Jones.

"But instead of the beatings and raping that I had to endure, her Captain led her into a life of piracy."

Ms. Jones had to admit that she could see the similarities between the two women's stories but couldn't see where her Captain was heading with the comparison.

"I'm not sure I understand what you're saying," she said.

"I think she would make an excellent addition to the crew." Mary told her First Mate, unable to take her eyes off Bonny. The cart had arrived in the square and the three pirates were now being led onto the gallows. Ms. Jones was stunned by Mary's statement.

"But Captain she's a pirate and has been given a death sentence!"

"She's only a pirate because of that man!"

Mary growled her voice full of venom as she glared at Rackham.

As for the pirate, he had just had the noose placed around his neck. He looked to Bonny and Read and said,

"Any last words of love before I die?"

"I am sorry to see you like this," Bonny told him.

"But if you'd fought like a man, you wouldn't be about to hang like a dog."

With that she turned her back on him and Calico Jack was sent on his last voyage.

# Chapter thirty-one.

Gallows: a wooden frame, usually made of two upright posts and a crossbeam with a noose attached, used to execute people by hanging. After hanging the pirates' bodies were normally hung on display in a gibbet.

"*W*hat do you mean you want us to rescue these women?"

Isabel said, absolutely dumbfounded by what Mary had just told her. After the hanging Mary and Ms. Jones had left the town square and returned to the Jenny's Revenge. On their journey Ms. Jones had explained that the only reason the two women had had a stay of execution was because they were quick with child.

"Then we have a chance to rescue Bonny." Mary stated.

"And Mary Read?" Ms. Jones asked.

"What of her. If we are to rescue one, why not rescue the other as well?"

Mary drew up short. She had gotten so enwrapped in Bonny's tale, so close as it was to her own, that she had learned nothing of Read. Back on the Jenny, Mary had called for her heads to meet in her cabin.

"I mean," Mary said in answer to Isabel's question.

"We should look to release them from their captors and make them part of the crew."

A string of obscenities burst forth from the Master-at-Arms, all in French so many in the room were spared their meaning.

"So, I thought the whole reason for bein' 'ere was to kill pirates?"

Anne said, her West Country accent giving her question an accusatorial tone.

"Now you're sayin' we should be recruiting 'em?"

"No." Mary said flatly.

"Not pirates, just these women."

"The women who were found guilty of piracy!" Isabel barked. "Those women."

"They only became pirates because that's where circumstance took them." Mary retorted.

"If the Captain that took me had asked me to join him as a pirate instead of taking me captive, I would have joined him in a heartbeat."

She paused to look each of them in the eye.

"I would have done anything for that man at the time."

"That may be true," Isabel continued to argue.

"But they have still sailed under a skull and crossbones."

"I know," Mary conceded. "But if we are to face Blackbeard, Bonny and Read may well be the key to our success."

That caused a moment of consternation in the room.

"And how do you think these women will make a difference?" Isabel asked.

"So far we have always laid in ambush," Mary explained. "From everything I've learned about Blackbeard, I'm not sure that we can rely on our usual tactics."

"But what difference will these women make?" Ms. Jones said, repeating Isabel's question. She was still convinced that Mary's sole reason for wanting Bonny was because their similar experiences and Read was just getting to come along for the ride.

"As you said Isabel, they have sailed under a skull and crossbones. These two women know exactly how to fight like pirates and how their ships operate."

"I think I get what you're sayin' Captain," Anne said.

"They might know somethin' we can use, but 'ow are we supposed to rescue them? We don't even know where they are."

"Well…" Ms. Jones interjected.

"We still have to see the Governor to see if Woodes Rogers has given us any orders. I'm sure that with a few subtle questions, their location could be found."

"That could work," Mary said.

"But once we've found them how do we get to them?"

"If I might Ma'am," Anne interrupted.

"Ms. Jones mentioned that the two of them are with child?"

"That's true Anne," Ms. Jones answered the woman's question.

"It's the only reason they weren't hung with Rackham."

"What does it matter if they are pregnant or not?"

Isabel blurted, her voice full of frustration. She couldn't believe they were actually discussing the rescue of these two pirates.

"I don't see how that gets us to them."

"Well," Anne said rubbing her chin in concentration. "If they're pregnant they'll probably need a midwife, so let's give them one."

"We don't have a midwife on the crew," Ms. Jones said slightly confused.

"We don't 'ave a midwife as such," Anne said wryly.

"But we do 'ave Rebecca and she's got all them books. I'm sure she could learn enough to bluff 'er way through."

"It's a good idea," Mary said. "But she's laying low, remember."

"Well that might be true," Anne went on.

"But the way I see it, the parts of town that Rebecca might be recognised in aint the part of town she'll be going to."

They all had to admit that she had a point.

"As usual Anne your wisdom has given us a plan."

Mary said and Anne blushed slightly at her kind words.

"Ms. Jones, you will go to see the Governor and find the whereabouts of Bonny and Read. Once we have that, Rebecca will go in as their midwife and find out if we can get them out without being noticed."

They all nodded in agreement and the plan was set.

# Chapter thirty-two.

Privateer: a ship that belongs to and is run by a person or company but is authorized by the government to engage in battle during war. Many privateers became pirates after peace was declared between Spain and England.

Once more Ms. Jones made the trip to the Governor's mansion, but this time there was no pirate trial to distract from her business at hand. Although she had seen him at the trial, this was to be her first-time meeting with the new Lieutenant Governor, and she was interested to see who had replaced Thomas Lynch. When she got to the mansion gates she went through the usual routine of when questioned, stating her business at the mansion and who she was there to see, before showing the letter from Woodes Rogers. She was then escorted through the grounds to the mansion. This time though, instead of being shown to the Governor's office, she was instead taken to see his deputy. The Deputy Governor sat behind an opulent desk strewn with what appeared to be shipping invoices. He was a large man with thick dark hair and a matching beard. He looked up from his work only when Ms. Jones came to a stop in front of his desk and the look on his face made it abundantly clear that he was not happy with the interruption.

"What do you want?"

He bit out, obviously of the opinion that his position elevated him above anyone who came before him. Ms. Jones didn't let it bother her and replied that she had come to see if there were any orders from Woodes Rogers for her Captain.

"Your Captain?"

The man said suddenly very interested in the woman stood before him. "You say that as if you're a part of the crew." The hairs on the back of Ms. Jones' neck bristled and she grew uneasy under the man's scrutiny.

"My husband is the Captain on a pirate hunting ship."

She said quickly thinking of a plausible story.

"You call your husband Captain?"

The Deputy Governor said clearly unconvinced.

198

"Do you sail with him then, is that why you call him Captain?"

Ms. Jones knew that it was still a commonly held belief that it was bad luck to sail with a woman as part of the crew, and she hurriedly continued fabricating her story.

"When my husband first set out, he was a simple deck hand on a merchant vessel," she told him.

"At the time we weren't married, but he promised that when he became a Captain we would be wed. We are now wed and so I call him my Captain."

"And the name of your *'Captain'*?" He asked, leaning back and stroking his beard. The stance was relaxed but his gaze was anything but. It said, "If you lie to me, I will know."

"Emmery," Ms. Jones said, keeping her eyes locked with his.

"Emmery Jones."

What the Deputy Governor didn't know was that Ms. Jones was telling him the truth, mostly. Emmery Jones was her husband's name and he had indeed promised to marry her, but it was when he got his commission to become an officer in the Royal Navy, not a Captain.

"I see," the Deputy Governor said, satisfied that she was telling him the truth.

"Well as a matter of fact, I do have some orders...."

He was interrupted mid-sentence by the door to his office came crashing open.

"Morgan!"

Hollered the man who stormed in and then stopped dead in his tracks at the sight of Ms. Jones. His eyes ran down the length of her and then back up again and Ms. Jones struggled to suppress a shudder. She couldn't help but feel that the man was picturing her naked.

"Well,"

He said, his gaze lingering on the swell of her chest even though there was nothing to see as she wore a heavy coat.

"Who do we have here?"

"This is Ms. Jones, Governor Vaughan."

Morgan answered the man's question.

"She came to collect her husband's orders from Woodes Rogers."

Governor Vaughan's face soured at the mention of the man's name.

"Your husband is a pirate hunter?"

Vaughan asked Ms. Jones, seemingly no longer interested in her physically.

"More of an informer Sir," she replied.

"We have lost much to those cut throats Sir, so he gives information to Woodes Rogers about their movements."

"Well madam,"

Vaughan said, snatching the sealed papers that Morgan held.

"This will be the last time you receive anything from Rogers through this office."

He thrust out the papers as if he were driving a blade through her. She took them and nonchalantly placed them into her pocket.

"I suggest," Vaughan continued.

"If you want anything further from Rogers, that you see him directly."

"Where might I find Governor Rogers?"

Ms. Jones asked as she genuinely had no idea.

"He has taken up residence in New Providence on Nassau."

Morgan informed her.

"Thank you Governor, Deputy Governor."

Ms. Jones said offering a slight bow to both and turned to leave. As she passed through the door, she couldn't help but hear Vaughan's words to Morgan.

"Henry, you have taken to many liberties this time."

She nearly stumbled at the man's name. Henry Morgan, the privateer was alive! The pirate who had raised Panama, had not only been spared from the gallows but had been made Deputy Governor of Port Royal, and she had been stood in front of him. Thankfully she had not been part of the boarding party that had boarded his ship, but it did explain his interest when she had mentioned 'her' Captain. As she walked across the mansions grounds towards the main gates Ms. Jones remembered that she still needed to find out the where Read and Bonny were being held. She stopped at the gates and asked the guards.

"Excuse me Sir, I was at the trial of those dreadful pirates yesterday. Could you possibly tell me what happened to those wretched women?"

The guard to her left, looking slightly amused at being called Sir answered.

"Don't you worry none Miss. They're being safely held at Marshallsea prison."

# Chapter thirty-three.

Democracy: the right to a form of government in which power is invested in the people as a whole. Pirate crews were brutal but fair, their Captains being elected by democratic vote. Pirate Captains only had unchallenged rule over their ship during times of war and could find themselves voted out if the crew were unhappy with them.

On her return to the Jenny's Revenge, Ms. Jones revealed the two pieces of information that she had learned at the Governor's mansion. She decided to start with the good news that she had learned the whereabouts of Read and Bonny's captivity.

"Excellent news Ms. Jones!"

Mary proclaimed, a smile spreading over her scarred face.

"Where's this prison to?" Anne asked.

"Up where Port Royal joins the mainland," Ms. Jones answered.

"So we're going to have to find a way of getting Rebecca there."

"Well," Anne mused.

"I reckon she'd 'ave to get a cab most of the way and then walk so as not to draw attention."

"What do you mean by not drawing attention?" Mary asked her.

"Well, you know," Anne replied.

"If Rebecca keeps showing up in a cab, they might get suspicious, what with her being a simple midwife."

"That's a good point," Ms. Jones said.

"How would a midwife afford a cab every day."

Mary nodded her head in agreement.

"As ever Anne," she said. "Your council has proven invaluable."

She looked around her cabin at her most trusted crew mates.

"So, does anybody have any ideas on how we get Rebecca into the prison to see them?" she asked.

"I could just walk up to the door," Rebecca said.

"Just walk up an' tell 'em why I'm there."

"It could work," Ms. Jones said contemplatively.

"After all they will just turn you away if they don't want to let you in."

"But what if they question you?" Mary asked, concerned

what might happen if the girl should be caught.

"What will you tell them?"

"I'll just tell 'em I'm doin' it out of the kindness of my heart." Rebecca answered trying to alleviate some of her Captains concerns.

"In fact, if I tell 'em I'm doin' it for the babies…"

"…they'll never doubt it." Anne finished the sentence.

"Men'll believe that kind of thing every time."

"Well then it's decided," Mary said.

"Was there anything else Ms. Jones?"

"I'm afraid there is," the First Mate answered.

"But you're not going to like it. Henry Morgan is alive."

"What!"

It was Mary who spoke, but Ms. Jones could see that the whole of the room was in shock at her news.

"How can that be?" Mary continued.

"We were told he'd been sent back to England to face trial."

"I don't know Ma'am. All I can tell you is that he's here and he's now the Deputy Governor."

Unbeknown to the crew of the Jenny's Revenge, when Morgan had gotten back to England, instead of being tried as a pirate, he'd been hailed as a hero. With that came a full pardon and a commission. A look of hatred flowed down Mary's face like a tsunami.

"I swore that I would kill that man for what he did to Panama," she said.

All of them thought that she was going to storm out to go and kill the man right there and then and Isabel even moved to block the door.

"There's nothing we can do right now," Ms. Jones cautioned.

"He's the Deputy Governor. Getting close to him will be impossible."

"You're right Ms. Jones," Mary said, still angry but her

initial rage had dissipated.

"We must bide our time and come up with a plan but getting to Morgan will be difficult not impossible. We will find a way."

# Chapter thirty-four.

Superstition: an irrational, but usually deep-seated belief in the magical effects of a specific action or ritual especially in the likelihood that good or bad luck will result from performing it. Sailors and pirates alike were very superstitious believing in all sorts including spirits. Davy Jones locker was high on their list. Often referring to the bottom of the sea, it also represented death, Jones being an evil spirit that preyed on sailors.

Getting Rebecca into the prison proved much easier than any of them would have believed it would be. As it turned out there was no midwife nor a doctor expected for the two pirate women. After Rebecca had explained why she was there and following an inspection of the contents of her bag, she had been taken to the two women's cells. On her first two visits she had been let in without question but kept under guard the whole time that she was with the pirate women. On her third visit however, she was confronted by the prison's Governor.

"You, midwife!" he barked whilst she inspected Read.
"The orders for these women are that they were to be afforded only food and water. So the question is, who are you?"

"I'm just a midwife milord." Rebecca said, her voice little more than a whisper.

"I 'eard that these women are with child and came to volunteer my services. Your men let me in Sir."

The prison Governor glared at his men.

"Did none of you think to question her, or to come and see me to see if she had permission to be here?"

The guards all stood at attention, their gazes fixed on the ceiling until one of them had the courage to step forward.

"We searched her bag Sir and she seemed legitimate."

"She seemed legitimate!" the Governor roared.

"Well that's all right then. She seemed legitimate."

With the speed of a striking cobra the Governor lashed out, delivering a backhanded blow to the man's jaw with such force that it knocked him to the ground. Rebecca retreated to the nearest corner of the room and curled into a ball. She wasn't actually scared but wanted to give the impression that she was and could easily be intimidated by somebody like the Governor. Turning to Rebecca the Governor offered her his hand.

"Come now, up you get young lady, no need for that sort of thing."

Rebecca took the proffered hand and got to her feet.

"I do not believe that these women deserve anything," he continued.

"But their unborn children are innocent of the mother's crimes and deserve a chance in this world."

"That's why I'm here Sir." Rebecca said gazing up into the Governors eyes.

"I can't have children of my own."

"Yes, yes," the Governor said clearly uncomfortable with where the conversation was heading.

"Let's not get ahead of ourselves. The state will decide what happens to the children."

"Yes Milord, sorry Milord," Rebecca said bowing her head submissively.

"So, can I continue to care for the women?"

"No."

The Governor replied flatly, confusing Rebecca after everything he had just said.

"You may continue to care for the unborn children that these women are carrying."

# Chapter thirty-five.

Larboard: The left side of a vessel. Changed to Port officially by the Royal Navy around 1844 to avoid the confusion between Starboard and Larboard when orders given.

*It* only took a week for the guards to stop paying attention to Rebecca. She visited the prison at a different time everyday telling the guards that it was because she was coming when she had spare time. In truth, she was taking note of the guards shift patterns and patrol times. The only times she couldn't get were at night, and as she could find no good reason to visit at night, but that was about to change. On her eighth visit Rebecca came in the evening hoping to learn what she needed but discovered two things she hadn't expected to, the first surprised her, the second saddened. As usual the guards greeted her and escorted her to the two pirate women. They weren't her favorite guards. These two, like so many, were pressed men. This made them unprofessional and predictable. One was always rough with her, both physically and verbally. It was evident that he despised both Read and Bonny and as such wasn't happy with the treatment that Rebecca was giving them. The other was a letch and Rebecca had felt his hands wondering more than once when he pretended to help her through doorways. As usual, once she was in with the women she was left alone. Mary had made it clear from the beginning that Bonny was to be the main focus of the rescue and so it was to her that Rebecca always went to first.

"Good evenin' Anne, 'ow are you and the baby today?" Rebecca asked.

She had started to develop a friendship with both of the women which she figured would make it easier to convince them to join the crew when it came time to bust them out. She went through her normal routine of taking heart rate and temperature, before moving on to examining Anne's stomach.

"I must say Anne," she said somewhat perplexed.

"I thought you would be showing more by now."

"Can I tell you a secret?" the pirate whispered, her Irish

accent thick with her low voice.

"You have shown me nothing but kindness when you didn't have to."

Rebecca smiled kindly at the woman. She recognised that she had earned Bonny's trust and if she played this just right, she would be able to convince the woman to join them with little difficulty.

"Well, I couldn't 'ave the two of you going without care." She said, placing a hand on Bonny's belly as she did.

"I'm not pregnant!"

Bonny blurted out as if this was the only way that such news could be broken. Rebecca snatched her hand back as if the action would change what she had just been told.

"I didn't want to die," Bonny continued with her confession.

"So, when Mary said she was with child I said I was as well."

Rebecca looked the woman in the eye to see if she could detect any deception in her words, but she could tell that the woman was telling the truth and was dumbfounded by her audacity.

"What was your plan for when you got found out?" she asked.

Bonny simply shrugged.

"I thought I might find a way to escape."

"Well I might be able to 'elp with that," Rebecca told her. Before anything else could be said, a howl of anguish and pain came from the direction that Mary Read was being held. Rebecca rushed to Read's cell and found her balled up on the floor. She clutched at her belly and as Rebecca knelt to examine the woman, she could see that her skin had a red blotchy rash, and she was running a fever. Further examination revealed that her glands were also swollen.

"What's the matter with her?" Bonny asked from the doorway of the cell. In her rush to get to Read's cell,

Rebecca realised that she had forgotten to close and bolt the door to Bonny's.

"I'm not sure," Rebecca answered.

"She's burnin' up and has a rash. If I didn't know better, I'd swear she's got Scarlet fever."

"What do you mean if you didn't know better?" Bonny asked, clearly confused by what she was being told about her crew mate.

"Well in order to get Scarlet fever," Rebecca explained. "She would have to have gotten it from someone else who has it."

"The guard who brings us our food didn't look to healthy last night." Bonny said.

"But if that's who she got it from, why didn't I?"

"It could be because she's pregnant and you're not." Rebecca answered and as she did so, she tried to get Read to drink some water. Try as she might though, the woman couldn't get any down.

"Is she dying?"

Bonny asked and then repeated more sharply, feeling Rebecca was ignoring her.

"Yes!"

Rebecca snapped. She'd torn a strip off Read's shirt and after soaking it with water, was using it to try and cool the woman's brow. Try as she might though, she couldn't get her temperature to come down. Read let out a strained sob and tried to talk, but with her glands being as swollen as they were, it came out as little more than a horse croak.

"Anne, I'm scared!"

Anne came into the cell and knelt beside her crew mate.

"You're going to be alright," she whispered.

Rebecca looked at her expecting to find the woman distraught at the prospect of losing a friend, but she saw instead a face contorted with anger.

"You were a good crewmate Mary."

Bonny continued, her voice soft and a total contrast to the hardness of her face. Read started to pant for air as her throat closed up further and Rebecca could see that the woman didn't have long to live.

"Help me make 'er comfortable." she told Bonny.

"What!" Bonny snapped.

"What do you mean get her comfortable?"

"She aint got long now," Rebecca said firmly.

"We need to make it look like she's sleeping."

"I don't get it, why?"

Bonny questioned, totally confused by what was being asked of her. Again the anger returned to her face.

"What's the point?"

"Why are you so angry?" Rebecca asked the woman.

"First Jack betrays me," Bonny hissed between clenched teeth.

"And now Mary's leaving me as well. How would you feel?"

She glared at her dying friend and Rebecca could see that she was channeling her sorrow into rage. Rebecca went to move Read but Bonny slapped her hands away.

"I'll do it!"

She snarled and then went about arraigning her dying crewmate so that she looked as though she were sleeping. Read had now slipped into unconsciousness so didn't protest to being manhandled. This wasn't the way Rebecca had wanted to get Bonny to join their crew, but she knew she had no choice. It was now or never.

"I think it's time that I told you the truth as to why I'm really 'ere."

Bonny didn't look up from what she was doing but replied none the less.

"You're a midwife, you told me already."

"No, that was just a way in," Rebecca confessed.

"So that we could get to see the two of you."

Bonny did stop what she was doing this time.

"What do you mean so 'we' could get to see the two of you?"

Rebecca started to feel nervous as Bonny suddenly looked dangerous in the confines of the cell, but she pressed on.

"I'm part of a crew on a ship called the Jenny's Revenge. We hunt pirates…."

Bonny was suddenly on top of Rebecca, pinning her to the floor by her shoulders.

"So you thought you'd come and kill us did you?"

"No!" Rebecca shrieked, stunned by the speed and strength of the woman.

"We want you to join us!"

The statement took Bonny by surprise, so much so that she stopped holding Rebecca's shoulders down but didn't get off of her.

"You came to get us to join you?" she said incredulously.

"Two pirates on the crew of a pirate hunting ship!"

At that she started laughing.

"Are you mad?" she said through chuckles.

"And what kind of crew sends a woman in, to get women to join their ship? Thought they'd be able to have their wicked way with us did they?"

"No. there are no men on our ship."

Rebecca told her and Bonny was so stunned she got off her and leant against the opposite wall.

"No men?"

Bonny said and Rebecca couldn't figure out if she were asking a question or just thinking out loud.

"No men," she replied anyway.

"Just those who've suffered, one way or another, at their hands. Those that were pirates anyway."

Bonny looked at the still form of her former crewmate.

At some point since Rebecca's proposition, the woman had passed away and she felt guilty that she hadn't noticed. The two of them had been through much together and she would miss her.

"So, how do you plan on getting me out of here?"

Rebecca got to her feet and looked down at Read. She nodded, happy with how the woman looked.

"First we have to make your bedding look like her." She told Bonny, nodding at the form of Read.

"And we have to move fast, the guards will be changing soon."

Rebecca had made a point of stopping and talking to the guards whenever she left the prison. This meant that they had become used to her distracting them. The two on at the moment were the easiest to distract. The letch always tried to get close to her in an attempt to get a sly touch in, whereas the angry one spent the short time chastising her for helping pirates. It was Rebecca's hope that the distraction would be enough that Bonny would be able to slip out unnoticed. Bonny was about to enter her cell when she turned to Rebecca, who was in the process of sliding the bolt on Reads cell and asked,

"Why do you want me to join you?"

"The Captain will explain everything," Rebecca told her. "For now, let's concentrate on getting you out of here."

They quickly arranged the straw that covered the cell floor into the rough shape of a person and covered it with the coarse blankets they had been provided with. Once done they closed and bolted the door before Rebecca took the lead and they worked their way towards the prison gates. Rebecca suspected the passageways would be clear as the guards choosing to believe that nobody could break-out neglected their patrols and was pleased to find she was correct. As she knew they would be, the guards stood by the gates not really guarding anything. With Bonny standing just out of sight, Rebecca made as if to walk out the gates but then turned back and started talking to the guards. As she had walked past them before turning back to talk to the guards, it meant that their full attention was on her with their backs towards the prison's interior. This allowed Bonny to slip from her hiding place and creep towards the gates. As she neared then guards, Rebecca subtly shifted her position so as to keep their backs to Bonny. Just as it looked as if she was about to slip out into the cover of the darkness outside the gates, Bonny paused to eye the guards' rifles. She then took a step in the direction of the guards, the move shocked Rebecca and as a result she inhaled sharply. Both the guards stopped what they were saying and stared at her. She quickly started coughing and clutched her chest with her right hand whilst appearing to reach for the wall behind her with her left. In actual fact, from where Bonny stood, she was pointing and waiving repeatedly to the gates. Finally, Bonny got the hint and slipped out into the night. After a while Rebecca joined her.

"Took your time." Bonny accused her as if she had somewhere important to be.

"Had to let them get me some water for that sudden cough I got."

Rebecca scowled at the woman, but it was lost in the darkness.

# Chapter thirty-six.

The pirate code: Articles of agreement raised by the crew, agreeing on the code of conduct for each ship. They were strictly adhered to and included rules for discipline, division of stolen goods and compensation for injuries.

Bonny paced back and forth in the Captain's cabin of the Jenny's Revenge. She had the presence of a caged tiger and all in the room were a little fearful of her, such was her reputation.

"So will you join us or not?" Mary asked.

Bonny stopped her pacing and turned to face Mary.

"I don't know," she confessed.

"It doesn't sit right with me, turning my back on my own kind."

"You mean pirates." Ms. Jones stated.

"Yes. I mean pirates."

Bonny answered, glaring at Ms. Jones as she did so.

"They are not your kind."

Mary said, standing as she addressed the woman.

"Take a look around you, we are your kind."

She turned as she said this, her sweeping gesture taking in the women in the room.

"Every member of this crew has been beaten, raped, orphaned or lost loved ones and livelihoods by those that you would call *'your kind'*."

She spoke with such passion that with every step forward, Bonny felt compelled to take one back.

"We are the same you and I. We both lost our heart to a Captain. Except where mine beat, raped and tried to kill me, your's turned you into a killer."

Bonny took in the faces of those in the room. Some, like Mary and Isabel, were disfigured by violence. Others, like Anne and Lucy, were still pretty but their eyes were haunted, and she could easily guess what had happened to these women. Her gaze settled on Rebecca, and she was reminded of how much danger the girl had put herself in, how much all these women had put on the line to help her escape. Something none of the pirates in all Port Royal had thought to do. She bowed her head in shame.

"What do you want from the likes of me?" she asked.

"We are going to hunt and kill Blackbeard." Mary said matter of factly.

Bonny's eyes literally bulged at Mary's statement.

"Are you mad!" she blurted.

"No." Mary answered in the same tone.

"I believe that with your help we can take on and defeat him."

"I'm not sure what you think I'll be able to do against a devil like Blackbeard." Bonny said, clearly stupefied by Mary's words.

"You've been with pirates, so you know how they fight. You know their methods and tactics, and that might give us the advantage." Ms. Jones told her.

"An' Blackbeard aint no devil," Anne joined in.

"He's just a man that acts like one."

"A man he may be," Bonny said.

"But it's still suicide to go up against him! Who put you up to this? Was it that Woodes Rogers? I heard the crew saying you worked for him."

"It was Blackbeard himself that '*put us up to this*', as you put it." Mary told her.

"The first time that he committed an act of piracy. As for Rogers, we no longer work for him."

After the plan to get Rebecca into the prison had been made and set into motion, Ms. Jones remembered the orders that Morgan had given her. Rogers wanted them to go in search of Hornigold as he hadn't returned from his business in New Spain. Rogers was concerned that something had happened to one of his top men and wanted them to find out what. They were to use their letter and his orders to get whatever they needed and leave immediately.

Unbeknown to Rogers, his orders gave them the perfect alibi for why they were in Port Royal and their sudden departure, removing them as suspect in the escape of Anne Bonny. Mary had the crew carry out the orders, at least for the first part. They replenished the Jenny's stores and armoury, telling all that would listen what their orders were and who they were from. The hope was that should Rogers ask, as far as anyone knew, the Jenny's Revenge had set sail in search of one Benjamin Hornigold. It was Mary and Ms. Jones's hope that should they ever happen to cross paths with Rogers again, they would simply report that they had been unable to find any trace of Hornigold or his ship. All they had left to do was to set sail and sever all ties with their would-be benefactor. Bonny considered this to be good news for her as her former husband had worked with Rogers and she had no desire to cross paths with either of them again. She smiled at Mary and said,

"Could I at least get a tour of the ship before I make my decision?"

Mary nodded her concession and she; Anne and Isobel escorted their newest potential crewmate around the Jenny. Bonny had to admit to herself that she was impressed by what she saw. It was when they came to the Demi-cannons though, that she was truly awestruck and let out a low whistle of appreciation.

"Where the hell did you get those?" she questioned.

"Working with Rogers had some advantages." Mary told her.

"They aren't very accurate…"

"But if yer side by side they'll cut straight through, BOOM!" Anne interrupted, finishing Mary's sentence.

"Okay Captain," Bonny said and held out a hand to shake.

"Looks like you got yourself a new crewman!"

Mary took the offered hand, receiving and giving a firm shake.

"Just out of curiosity," Bonny asked.

"If I hadn't agreed to join you, what then?"

By way of answer Isabel gave her a toothless smile and patted her pistol.

# Chapter thirty-seven.

Pirate treasure: there is little evidence that pirates ever buried their treasure. In truth pirates would steal anything thought to hold value, from spices to silks and even slaves. Any 'Booty' obtained during raids would then be sold on and the money would then be divided between the crew, who would more often than not squander it on rum, gambling and women.

They set sail on the next available tide. Although they had been given the perfect cover story for their departure from Port Royal, Mary was keen for them not to appear too eager to leave. News of the prison break had started to be heard on the streets and the last thing they needed was the attention of the authorities. Mary stood on the half deck and looked back at Port Royal as they left. She could taste the bitter bile of frustration that came from knowing once again she was sailing away from Henry Morgan and he still lived. She would have vengeance for the people of Panama, but for now Ms. Jones was right, they couldn't simply kill him without suffering the consequences. Especially now that he was Deputy Governor.

"Good morning Captain!"

Bonny called from the main deck snapping Mary out of her ruminations.

"Good morning Anne," Mary returned the greeting and joined the woman on the lower deck.

"I take it you slept well?"

"Better than a prison cell." Bonny replied with a sardonic grin.

"So. Now that you've got me, what would you have me do?"

"I want you to take a look at how we do things." Mary told her.

"Once we're away from prying eyes, we'll show you everything we've used against the pirates we've fought so far. Then I want you to tell me if you think any of it will work against Blackbeard."

The next few days were consumed with drill practice. Bonny would watch each of the parties and then give her opinion. This did not go without friction between herself and the party leaders. In particular was the boarding party and Isabel. After demonstrating their tactic of hiding in the rigging and swinging down to board an enemy ship, Bonny had laughed at them.

"You don't actually expect that t' work do ya?"

Isabel, temper barely under control, told the former pirate that it did work, especially when used with the decoy party, and had been used to great success against Stede Bonnet and his crew.

"You were lucky," Bonny scoffed.

"For starters, Bonnet was a bloody awful pirate, and his crew weren't much better."

That had been the last straw for Isabel who flew at Bonny. Used to having to defend herself from sudden attacks, Bonny fended off the blows delivered by Isabel before returning her own. By the time Mary came from her cabin to break it up, both women were bloodied and bruised.

"Both of you. My cabin. Now!"

Once all three were in the confines of the cabin Mary whirled on the two combatants.

"What the hell was that?"

"She didn't like my criticisms." Bonny said, nodding her head at Isabel.

Isabel looked as though she were about to attack Bonny again, but a withering glare from Mary convinced her otherwise.

"She laughed at our boarding technique." She growled instead.

"You are supposed to be advising us on how best to beat Blackbeard." Mary told Bonny, her tone making it clear there were to be no interruptions.

"You are not here to poke fun at the crew. Everything we have shown you these past few days has been tried and tested, some more than others, against real pirates and found to work."

"Well, that maybe true for other pirates but none of it will work against Blackbeard." Bonny said matter of fact.

"He comes in all guns blazing every time he sees prey."

"Are you saying none of our methods will work?" Mary questioned, shocked at what she was being told.

"Well maybe your decoy party, but it will need some work." Bonny said with a shrug.

"What do you mean?" Isabel asked, still angry with the woman, but she was back in control of herself.

"See, Blackbeard deals in fear and reputation. When a crew spots his flag, and his shots start raining down around them, most men are gonna need new britches."

Bonny told them, all the while wearing a look akin to respect for the man's methods.

"So, surrender is your only option." Mary said, shaking her head as if the very concept was preposterous.

"Or death. I mean you could try to fight, but you'd lose, and then you'd die."

"So how will the decoy party make a difference?" Isabel asked.

"If what you say is true, I don't know what you think they will be able to do."

"Like I said, it'll need some work." And with that she looked at Isabel a genuine smile.

"And if they all fight like this one," she said to Mary with a wink.

"We should have no problem at all."

The next few days saw the Decoy and Boarding parties working together on Bonny's new plan for them.

Bonny was intrigued by their Katars and after a short lesson with Isabel in its use, confessed to preferring the blade over her old cutlass. From the boarding party she singled out the members that had suffered beatings to the face and had the scars to prove it. The others she moved to join the Decoy party. She then watched them all sparring with training blades but after only a few minutes bought them to a stop.

"Enough!" she screeched, extremely agitated.

"What's with all the tap-tap-tap rubbish!"

She shouted at them, referring to the training patterns they had just been doing.

"You're fighting pirate's ladies! They fight dirty and with pure rage. If you're hoping to survive against Blackbeard's crew, you need to bloody well do the same. Bite. Kick. Spit. If you see an opening, use it. Hell, if you think it will give you an advantage, bare your chest! Now get back to it!"

She was pleased to see that the women had taken her words onboard and were now sparring with greater vigor.

"How do they fare?"

Ms. Jones asked Bonny, joining her from the gun deck where she had been watching the crews run through their loading drills.

"They have the heart," Bonny told her. "They just need more aggression."

"Remember, these women aren't the pirates you're used to working with." Ms. Jones told her.

"Maybe not, but they need to learn to fight like them if we're to stand a chance."

# Chapter thirty-eight.

Rum: A potent alcoholic drink made from sugar cane or molasses in the Caribbean. Back in the 18$^{th}$ century pirates and the RN would douse gunpowder with rum and if it still ignited it was 'proof' that the alcohol content was high enough. It was rumored the pirate Blackbeard used to add gunpowder to his calling it a mind blast.

They sailed the shipping lanes between Tortuga and Port Royal at a gentle clip. Flying British colours and a merchant flag, they hoped to present themselves as an appealing target for Blackbeard and his crew, who were known to prey upon such ships who sailed these lanes.

"The weathers starting to turn." Rose told Ms. Jones. Both stood on the half deck, Rose checking their bearings against the charts they had obtained from Stede Bonnet to ensure they stayed in Blackbeard's hunting grounds, Ms. Jones keeping watch. Ms. Jones looked to where the navigator had indicated and saw there was indeed a storm brewing on the horizon.

"Let us hope we only encounter the storm or Blackbeard." She said.

"I don't think we could take on both."

Rose nodded her head in agreement and then took bearings on the storm with her sextant. Ms. Jones went to the Captain's cabin to report the impending storm and found Mary, Bonny, Anne, Lucy and Isabel discussing the plan for taking on Blackbeard.

"Sorry to interrupt Ma'am," she said. "Just reporting a storm possibly heading our way on the horizon."

"Very good Ms. Jones," Mary replied to her first mate. "Please join us. We were just discussing with Anne [Bonny] all that we have learned about Blackbeard."

"What do you know about his crew?" Bonny asked as Ms. Jones took her place at the table.

"We know they're as scared of him as we are." Lucy told her.

"So they'll do anything he tells them to do."

"Who was that one that Bonnet mentioned in whispers?" Ms. Jones asked Mary.

"Ah yes I remember. He seemed scared to even mention his name. What was it Ms. Jones, do you remember?"

"Caesar!" Ms. Jones said with a sudden flash on remembrance.

"Black Caesar."

"Black Caesar!" Bonny gasped.

"Who's this Caesar that's got everyone scared to even say 'is name?" Anne asked.

"If what they say about him is true, he's an animal." Bonny told them and then proceeded to tell them all that she had heard about him. Caesar had once been an African Chieftain who had been fooled into slavery. During the crossing from Africa the ship had fallen foul to a storm and Caesar was freed by one of the ship's crew who he had befriended. From there, he and his rescuer entered into a life of piracy. Posing as shipwrecked sailors they would overpower their saviors before helping themselves to what they wanted. A life on the high seas had soon followed with Caesar the Captain of his own ship and crew. It was rumored that he had a secret hideout on an island somewhere near Florida where he kept his captives. The women became part of his harem and were offered out to his crew and guests to do with as they pleased. The men, if not killed instantly for sport, were used for ransom to further his great wealth. All he left on the island with no provisions of any kind whilst he was away. Described as a mountain of a man with strength and intelligence to match, it wasn't hard to see why Blackbeard had taken him on.

"Let us pray then." Ms. Jones said.

"That the rumors are just that, rumors."

"SAILS!" came a cry form a deckhand as she came barging in through the cabin door. She came to a halt, looking startled by the room's assembly.

Finally her gaze came to rest on Mary.

"Sorry Ma'am," she stammered, "but there's sails coming over the horizon."

Racing out onto the upper deck Mary saw a gaggle of the

231

crew gathered on the starboard rail and moved to join them. She could see that they were looking to the aft quarter and after a quick scan of the horizon, could just make out the silhouette of a ship hiding in the storm. She pulled out her spyglass and attempted to get a better look.

"Can you tell who it is yet Captain?" Ms. Jones asked, joining Mary at the rail.

"No, still too far out." Mary replied.

"But who else could it be out here."

"Yes Ma'am." Ms. Jones nodded in agreement.

"I'll ready the crew."

She turned and bellowed over the rising wind,

"All hands to quarters!"

"You 'eard 'er!" Anne cried taking up the call.

"Everyone into positions!"

The crew was a hive of activity in an instant. They were prepared for this moment but only so far. Cannons still needed to be primed and the decoy party dressed. The storm had picked up, but it was still dry and Mary hoped that it would remain so, otherwise it could look conspicuous that their passengers were all up on deck. She turned back to the approaching ship and could now see through her spyglass that they were hoisting their colours. And there it was, a black flag with a white skull accompanied by a blood red one, no quarters given.

"It's him!" she yelled. "It's him!"

The crew paused a heartbeat and Mary could feel the waves of fear pouring off of them. To their credit, they quickly returned to their preparations and once again, Mary felt a sense of pride swell in her chest. They could do this, they could defeat the infamous Blackbeard. The decoy and boarding parties were the first to take their positions. The intent and hope was that to anyone observing them from a distance, they would appear to be a merchant vessel with passengers; and passengers meant wealth. The decoy party were dressed in their usual attire of fine dresses and corsets. The boarding party on the other hand were dressed in one of two ways. Those with the scared-up faces were dressed in the uniform of a merchant sailor whilst others were dressed in the fine shirts and trousers of gentlemen. All had been acquired through various means including theft from washing lines. Mary knew that Anne would be making sure that all preparations below deck would be getting squared away, so moved to join Amy at the helm. She had been assured by Bonny, who was below decks helping with the preparations, that Blackbeard's ship the Queen Anne's revenge would fire upon them but only in so far as to scare and disable. As they closed into around a mile of them, the first shot was fired. It fell short, but Mary felt that was its intent.

"Helm, make it appear as though we intend to evade and flee." She ordered.

"All hands on deck, time to start looking panicked."
On Mary's orders all those on the upper deck started their performance. Those dressed as women started to scream and hugged those dressed as gentlemen giving the impression of scared travelers. Those dressed as sailors moved to the rigging and made out as if they couldn't decide between dropping the sails or putting on more. Amy put the Jenny hard to larboard as another warning shot splashed beside them. She continued to weave the ship about making as if they were heading for the safety of the nearest port. Shots continued to rain down around them, but as the Queen Anne's revenge closed the gap further, the shots started to sail between the rigging. Then their luck ran out and a shot tore through their mainsail and combined with the storm winds, it split wide open. Although not completely without sails, their forward speed was greatly reduced, and the pirates quickly closed the remaining distance between them. The rain came lashing down as the

Queen Anne's revenge came up on their starboard quarter. Without even bothering to come fully alongside, the pirate boarders swung or jumped across the gap to attack. The decoy and boarding party of the Jenny's Revenge allowed the first of the pirates to come fully aboard, keeping up their pretense of being terrified. Only when feet were fully on deck did they let loose. Blunderbusses were fired tearing apart those pirates in the lead, showering those behind in the blood and ichor of their crew mates. The Jenny's boarding party then went toe to toe with those that had survived the initial slaughter with pistols and Katars, joined by the decoy party who were similarly armed. Many fell on both sides and the deck was soon slick with blood and rainwater. As the Queen Anne's revenge continued to pull up alongside, boarders continued to hurl themselves between the two ships, eager to join in the fight. A giant of a man landed on the main deck, bare of chest, his onyx skin shimmered in the downpour. One of the Jenny's own boarding party quickly moved to take him on, but his cutlass easily parried the slash from her Katar. His return blow almost cleaved the woman in two, from shoulder to hip, such was the power in the man's arms. Black Caesar had arrived on the Jenny's Revenge and quickly set about bringing death to her crew. As the battle above deck waged on, down in the gun deck the crew sat with an uneasy feeling of incompetence. The Queen Anne's revenge had come alongside but not enough for them to bring their big guns, the Demi-cannons, into play. It felt to them that Blackbeard had some kind of sixth sense that told him not to draw up fully. Anne raced down into the gun deck from where she had been spying on the action through a crack in the door that led to the upper deck.

"All spare hands to arms!" she ordered.

"What's going on up there?"

Bonny demanded, Katar in hand and clearly frustrated at

being left out of the action. Mary had decided that it was best that she stay out of sight unless needed, just in case she be recognized.

"I think it's Black Caesar!" Anne told the former pirate. "He's killing everyone in his path!"

Without waiting for orders or the rest of the crew, Bonny raced up the stairs to join the melee. She shoulder barged the door on to the main deck only to slip on the blood and rain coating the deck. She landed on her back cracking her head on the hard wooden boards, causing her to black out for a second. When she came back around it was to the hulking form of Caesar looming over her. He laughed deep and heartily before raising his cutlass high overhead to deliver a killing blow. Before he could however, the smile slipped from his face, and he started blinking rapidly before toppling backwards to crash down on the deck. Bonny raised her head to look at the sprawled form of Caesar, totally confused as to how she was still alive. There protruding from his nose, almost comically if not for the situation, was a crossbow bolt. Rolling onto her belly and looking back in the direction she had come from, Bonny could see Anne crossbow in hand grinning at her.

"Yer welcome." The Quartermaster said. "Now pick yerself up and get back in the fight!"

Bonny scrambled to her feet and with an enraged scream tore her shirt open to expose her breasts. The distraction was more than enough to allow her to plunge her blade deep into the first pirate she came to and the second. Although the tactic worked, she was the only one to employ it. Unfortunately, even with the spare hands and Caesar removed from the action, the crew of the Jenny were soon overwhelmed by the difference in numbers when it came to crews. Blackbeard's men soon had them rounded up on the main deck and Mary had to concede defeat. Only then did Blackbeard's ship come fully alongside them. Ropes were tossed over to secure the two ships side by side and a boarding plank lowered. Then the man and legend, self-proclaimed pirate king appeared. Blackbeard leapt up to stand on the plank, his eyes malevolent.

"Bring me the Captain of this cursed vessel!"

His voice boomed like thunder. Mary stepped forward and two of his pirates grabbed her. They manhandled her more than was necessary and forced her onto the boarding plank to stand before their Captain.

"This truly is a cursed vessel if it has a woman for its Captain." Blackbeard growled.

"A woman who thought she could take on me and survive!"

"They're all women!" one of his crew called out with surprise.

Now that the battle was over and the pirates were able to get a proper look at the crew of the Jenny's Revenge, a few even stepped away from them.

"It aint right Captain!"

Another piped up but quickly quietened up again when Bonny, breasts still proudly exposed, gave her the full extent of her glare.

"You're right men!" Blackbeard agreed

"The sea is no place for a woman, and a ship crewed by them is nothing but bad luck."

He grinned at Mary, but there was no warmth in it. Instead, he looked like he'd just told a joke that only he knew the punch line to.

"I'll tell you what, I'll make you an accord."

With that he drew his cutlass.

"If you can beat me in a fair fight here and now, I'll let you and yer sea witches go."

"I'll make you a counteroffer." Mary said, surprising herself with the strength of her words.

"GUNS!"

She hollered and silently prayed that the gun crews were

ready below. On the gun deck there had been some confusion about what they should do. Their usual routine had been thrown into disarray when they had boarded early, and Blackbeard had then refused to present himself broadside and when he had they knew it was too late to open fire. Upon hearing their Captains order however, repeated throughout the deck, they hauled on the gun tackles pulling cannons hard up against their bulwarks. At the same time the lines to the gun ports were hung upon. To Blackbeard it appeared that the hull of the Jenny's Revenge had burst open and spewed out its deadly spines like some kind of sea creature.

"What you see below me Captain are two 32-pound Demi-cannons and four 18 pounders." It was Mary's turn to smile.

"All are primed and ready to blow out the side of your ship."

The rain had stopped and the slow matches in Blackbeard's hair now created a haze around the pirate's head. All the while his gaze burned through, and such was its ferocity Mary thought her heart might burst with fright. Through it all though she managed to keep a smile on her face.

"Well it looks like we're at a bit of an impasse."

Blackbeard said, and as he did the intensity of his gaze vanished and it was as if he and Mary were having a civil conversation about the weather.

"Although it's true that at your order you could destroy my ship, my men would simply slaughter you and your crew and take yours."

Mary nodded her head in agreement with the pirate, but her smile never wavered.

"That maybe as true Captain." She said.

"But with your ship destroyed the remainder of my crew would then be free to come above decks to aid in the defence of their ship."

"Well then, I believe it's time to put a new offer on the table."

Blackbeard said again with his cold smile and the intensity had returned to his eyes.

"As I have no desire to lose my ship, nor you your life or that of your crew."

Mary was about to interrupt with a protest, but a nod from Blackbeard made her look in the same direction.

Unbelievably Black Caesar was picking himself up off the deck, the bolt from Anne's crossbow still protruding from nose. The giant pulled it free causing a cascade of blood to pour down his front. It looked as if he were about to pick up where he'd left off, but a look and a hand gesture from his Captain was enough to still the savage beast.

"As I said, you have no desire to lose your life or crew."

"So what's your offer?" Mary asked warily, returning her attention to Blackbeard.

"Well as it turns out I'm in the market for a new wife, owing to the fact that the last one…. passed away."

He looked at the crew of the Jenny as if at a cattle market.

"I'm sure you can spare one of your crew?"

Mary was horrified at the suggestion. She'd put this crew together because of what men like Blackbeard had done to them. There was no way she was going to simply hand one of them over to become wife to this man.

"I find your offer to be vile and degrading!" she spat.

"Well then, it looks like it's back to plan A." Blackbeard said nonchalantly. Mary could hear the breath of Caesar growing heavy and fast as if building towards an explosion.

"I'll do it!"

Both Mary and Blackbeard turned to where the crew of the Jenny stood surrounded by Blackbeard's men.

"Who said that?" Mary demanded.

It was Ms. Jones who stepped forward.

"No. absolutely not." Mary told her First Mate.

"We don't have much of a choice Ma'am."
Ms. Jones replied, moving past Blackbeard's men with the intension of joining their Captain on the boarding plank.
Mary jumped down from where she stood on the boarding plank to block the woman's progress.
"Come now Captain." Blackbeard taunted.
"She's right, you don't have much choice."
With that he looked up and Mary felt inclined to do the same, following his gaze to where it settled on their tattered mainsail.
"After all, you're going nowhere fast. So long as we evade those cannons of yours…"
He spread his arms wide, and an equally wide sardonic grin spread across his face.
"And I like this one, she looks like she has spirit!"
"If you dare hurt her!" Mary snarled at the pirate.
Blackbeard let out a chuckle, but if anyone had looked closely through the haze of the long matches, they would have seen that he was surprised by the venom in the woman stood before him.
"I promise, Captain to Captain, that you have my word that she won't be harmed."
He gave her a little bow of respect, but Mary couldn't help but feel that he was mocking her.
"Now if you don't mind, times getting on and we must be going."
"Fine." Mary said, resigned to the situation she found herself in.
"Take your men and go."
She turned to Ms. Jones and hugged her fiercely.
"Don't let them hurt you." She whispered in her ear.
"Take your own life if you have to."
Strange Mary thought that that was exactly what she had stopped the woman doing when they had first met. Now her last words, to one of her closest friends, were to suggest

that she should do just that. They parted and Ms. Jones traversed the plank to be scooped into an embrace by Blackbeard. Then his men started to return to their ship one by one. As Caesar passed, he paused and spat at Mary's feet.

"I wouldn't even take one of you's sea witches for ma hareem!"

He gurgled through the blood from his nose.

With all aboard, the plank withdrew, and the lines were cut.

"Raise sails and make sure to stay clear of those bloody cannons!" Blackbeard ordered.

They had lost and not just the battle. Mary looked over at Ms. Jones. She stood proud and tall, refusing to be intimidated. Looking back at Mary as the divide between them grew, she smiled.

"Farewell Captain." she said before being dragged out of sight.

# Chapter thirty-nine.

The red flag: when used by pirates meant "no quarter given", or no mercy would be shown, and no life would be spared. Commonly used by pirates before the invention of the Jolly Rodger.

There was a great deal of work to accomplish in the days that followed their battle with Blackbeard. First they had to deal with the dead. The pirates were cast unceremoniously over the rails. The fallen crew of the Jenny were moved from where they had been slain with tender respect. It is traditional for those buried at sea to be wrapped in the colours of their native country. As the Jenny's Revenge sailed under no flag and her crew hailed from all points of the compass, the dead were respected by being wrapped in the remains of the damaged mainsail. It seemed only fitting that that a part of the ship that had united them in life, would now embrace them for all eternity in death. Mary headed the ceremony, as was only right of a ship's Captain, but it was one of the few times that the crew had seen her outside of her cabin since the loss of Ms. Jones. The upper deck had been in need of a scrubbing after the battle. Once the rain had stopped the deck had started to dry out, but with the rainwater gone the blood-stained deck had started to grow sticky. The heat of the day had also caused it to smell, and the stench of death was a constant reminder of what they had lost. Luckily there was an abundance of seawater to be had so cleaning and disinfecting the decks wasn't a problem. As Anne inspected the crew's work with Bonny, she thought out loud.

"There 'as to be a way to stop it gettin' so slippery?"

After all, she mused now silently in her mind, poor Anne [Bonny] had nearly lost 'er life to that Black Caesar. Would 'ave to if I 'and't shot 'im in the face.

"Sand." Bonny stated.

Anne looked at her quizzically, completely at a loss as to what the former pirate was saying.

"When I sailed with Jack Rackam and his crew, they used to sprinkle it over the decks to soak up the blood." Bonny explained.

"Oh, really." Anne said looking slightly embarrassed.
"I thought all them buckets of sand was for putting fires out."

"Well that too." Bonny said with a smile.
"But mostly for sanding the decks."

Finally the mainsail was replaced with their only spare. When all the work was finished, Anne took it upon herself to tell Mary that they were ready to return to port. But when she went to knock on the door of the Captain's quarters, she discovered that she didn't have the courage to face her alone. So she gathered Isabel, Lucy and Rebecca together. She figured that as they all had important roles on the Jenny, they should all report the ship's condition. At the last moment she grabbed Bonny to come with them as well, figuring that if they couldn't get the Captain to respond then perhaps she could. They knocked but didn't wait for a response before entering. The cabin was dark with all the shutters closed. Mary sat at the table in the centre of the room. The table was bare save for her hands which rested limply upon it. She stared into nowhere and didn't acknowledge or even seem to notice that she had visitors.

"Um, Captain?" Anne said trying to get her attention.
"I've got the rest of the team leaders with me to talk about the ship."

"I've failed you." Mary croaked as if she hadn't used her voice in days, her gaze remaining firmly fixed on nowhere.

"Well that aint true!" Anne told her finding, herself as the spokesman of the group.

"But it is." Mary replied and this time she did look at them. Her eyes were bloodshot and red rimmed, and it was easy to see she had been crying by the smearing down her cheeks. The glaze in the woman's eyes told them that she hadn't been sleeping either.

"When I recruited you all," Mary went on, "I promised you a safe haven and revenge."

She returned to staring into nowhere.

"But I failed you. We lost so many in that fight and I handed Ms. Jones over to the very people I promised you all refuge from."

"Oh, boo hoo!" Bonny spat out before anyone could say anything.

"So you lost people. They knew what they were getting into when you offered them a place on this ship."

She looked around her at those gathered in the room, her eyes boring into theirs as her gaze passed them by.

"You all knew this, didn't you?"

"Aye." They all answered in union.

"As for Ms. Jones." Bonny continued.

"She did what needed to be done for the good of the crew. So don't be disrespecting her decision with yer self-pity and wallowing!"

"How dare you speak to the Captain like that!"

Isabel growled and looked as if she were ready to draw her blade in defence of her Captain's honour.

"No!" came the firm voice of Mary.

"She's right, I have been sitting here in self-pity when I should have been out with the crew."

She rose and walked around the table to join the other women. Clasping a hand on Bonny's shoulder she said,

"Thank you Anne [Bonny]. Your blunt words were exactly what I needed. Keep up the good work."

Releasing Bonny's shoulder, she swept her gaze over them all with a grateful smile.

"Thank you, all of you, for picking up my slack. Now I believe you were going to tell me about the condition of the Jenny?"

For the next hour, each took it in turns to report their area of responsibility and the condition each was in.

During the reports Mary had returned to her seat and invited them all to take a seat with her. With the reports done, she leaned back in her chair and steeped her fingers in front of her face.

"Well, I think you've all done a fine job." She told them. "But there are still a few things that need to be done." They looked at her quizzically, sure they had missed nothing.

"With the absence of Ms. Jones on the ship I'll be needing a new First Mate."

She turned to Anne and smiled.

"Congratulations Anne, the position is yours."

Anne looked as shocked as when she had first been offered a position on the crew.

"What!Captainno!Ithinkyermakinamistake!" her words came out in one long word.

"No mistake Anne." Mary laughed.

"You have become the heart of the crew. Nobody knows them or is more respected by them than you."

The former bar wench blushed at her Captain's words, and then frowned.

"If I'm to be the First Mate, then who's gonna be the Quartermaster?"

Mary turned to Bonny.

"Anne [Bonny], I think that you have proven yourself to be a member of this ships company. If you want it, the position is yours."

"It's true, I've felt a part of this crew as like no other." Bonny said. She looked to each of them before continuing. "If they'll have me, I'll take the job."

"A vote it is then." Mary said with a nod.

"All in favor of Anne Bonny being the new Quartermaster of the Jenny's Revenge say aye."

The vote was unanimous.

"In that case, Quartermaster it is!" Bonny said giving them each a nod of gratitude.

"The last thing we need to decide…" Mary pondered

245

"Is where do we head for?"

"Can we not just return to Port Royal?" Rebecca asked.

"No, I don't believe we'll be able to return there for some time." Mary answered the girl.

"Although nobody there will find out what happened to Hornigold, we took the Kings provisions to go out and find him. If we return now, they will most likely believe that we didn't carry out Rogers's orders and accuse us of theft. That means Nassau is out as well."

"What happened to Hornigold?" Bonny asked.

"We killed him and his crew." Isabel answered nonchalantly.

"Oh!" Bonny said with surprise.

"Well, good job and good riddance."

"So, where to go?" Mary said, steeping her fingers once more.

"What about that chart with the island on it that you an' Ms. Jones found?" Anne asked excitedly.

"You know, the one from that Stede Bonnet's ship." Again, Bonny looked at them all, but this time her eyes were full of respect for her new ship mates.

"Well remembered Anne." Mary said and rose to get the chart in question.

"We need somewhere to lay low and a little-known island like that might be just the place we need."

"So where is this place then?" Bonny asked.

"It's in a nest of islands near Florida." Mary replied, unrolling the chart to show its location, and getting a frown from Bonny in reply.

"Is there a problem?" she asked.

"No, well maybe." Bonny replied.

"As I remember hearing it, that's Black Caesar's hunting grounds. Or it was before he joined up with Blackbeard."

"So do you think this island 'as something to do with Caesar then?" Anne quizzed the woman.

"Well now I couldn't say." Bonny answered, but she could feel the burn of curiosity building in her gut.

"You heard him as he left the ship." Isabel said.

"He wouldn't take us for his harem. Maybe this island is his secret hideout?"

"We should go!" Anne blurted out not bothering to hide her excitement.

"Who knows what we will find there!"

"Exactly." Isabel scolded the woman.

"Who knows indeed? We should be cautious if we are to go there."

"Well our options are limited." Bonny said blatantly ignoring the French woman.

"I think we should take a look. What say's you Captain!"

Mary pursed her lips and her brow furrowed in deliberation. She knew she should agree with Isabel, but with Caesar away with Blackbeard…

"I think we should take a look." She said finally.

Both Anne's looked delighted with the decision, but Isabel threw her hands up in consternation. It was Rebecca's words, quiet but hard hitting that bought the room back down, silencing both Anne's excitement and ceasing Isabel's argument before it could begin.

"We need somewhere that the crew can heal. Not just from the wounds inflicted by Blackbeard and his crew. But from the loss of our fallen comrades. If this island can give us that, then I'm all for it."

They all sat in silence for a moment as Rebecca's words sank in. it was Mary who finally broke it.

"Well said Rebecca, well said." She paused to look at each of them in turn before continuing.

"We will go to this mysterious island, but Isabel is right we need to be cautious. We're in no condition for a fight. Hopefully it will provide the solace we so badly need, but if there is so much as a whiff of trouble, we'll turn tale and find somewhere else. Agreed?"

"Aye!" They chorused and gave the table a single bang with their hands.

# Chapter forty.

Grog: a drink enjoyed by pirates and sailors alike. Consisting of one-part rum two parts water it was used as a way of stopping the fresh water turning brackish. Sugar and lime were introduced at a later point to improve the taste.

*H*e sat quietly in the corner of the tavern, using the shadows that naturally gathered there to hide his face. He had considered himself to be handsome once, but that was before he had been disfigured by a belaying pin. The blow had also damaged his eye, filling it with blood so that it was now almost completely black. Now when people looked at him, they shrank back from his demonic visage. From the shadows he eavesdropped on the tales being told by the tavern's patrons, regardless of how far-fetched they seemed. He'd heard snippets of tales of late, all with the same detail that had caught his attention. So he now made a point of listening out for those same snippets, hoping to hear the whole tale. Across the room, Blackbeard and his crew were celebrating and raising merry hell. The self-proclaimed king of the pirates had just been wed to his latest in a long string of wives. He presumed that it was she that sat beside Blackbeard now. She was older than he would have expected, having seen the young wenches the pirate normally sat upon his lap. She sat proper too, straight backed and refined. He wondered where the old sea dog had found her, but as he watched from his vantage point, he noted how none of the crew dared look at her directly as if they feared what might happen if they did. The drinks flowed and songs were being sung and before long the stories started to be told. Tales of strength, tales of bravery and before long the tale that he had waited so long to hear. "Not bad ay Captain!" one particularly drunk crewman called out.

"We might not have come away with any plunder, but we got a good fight, and you got a new wife!"

"To the Captain's wife!"

Someone toasted and they all chugged at the contents of their mugs before laughing heartily.

"I still think we could've taken 'em."

An unseen crewman said sulkily.

"After all, they was only women!"

"What d'ya mean they was only women?" Said a sailor from another crew.

"Aint no women on any crew, that's bad luck so it is!"

"That's right." Came a voice from the bar.

"Jack Rackham sailed with two of them and look what happened to him!" came yet another voice.

"Well, these was women and I'm tellin' ya that they crewed the whole damn ship!"

Shouted the crewman, angry that his words weren't being believed and stood to emphasise the point. The tavern fell silent at his words.

He sat in his corner, and he needed to know more, needed to hear the whole story.

"Why don't you tell us about it then?"

His voice was course and thin from where he had once inhaled nothing but sea water trying not to drown. The crewman looked to Blackbeard for permission and received a single nod.

"Right, pin 'em back and listen in. we sailed with a storm at our back, following us like an ill omen. There it sat, a three masted galleon of Spanish build, wide in beam and low in the water. Easy pickings says we. She be flying merchant colours and hauling passengers."

He lent forward leaving his shadows behind, such was his eagerness to hear more.

"We fire on 'er to give 'er a scare and she tries to run, but we take out her mainsail so compared to us she's dead in the water! We can see the decks now and they're thick with Gentlemen and ladies huddling in fear, and there's us thinking, here be some easy pickings."

The tavern was silent, patrons and staff alike, all hanging on the crewman's words. He looked over to Blackbeard's wife and could see her eyes were screwed shut as if she were reliving the crewman's tale as he told it. Each and every word, painted on the back of her eyelids.

"So as soon as we're in close quarters we're away and over not waiting for boarding planks, just swinging from the rigging! Before our very eyes they changed, them ladies bent over and hell's fire bursts out of them as they do, killin' those first over in an instant! And those Gents weren't no gents either! No, they were sea witches armed tooth and nail and they could fight! They started cutting' us down left and right with these weird blades that looked like they grew right out of their hand's. But we 'ad the numbers and soon rounded 'em up. Then our ship she pulls alongside, and boarding planks n ropes hold us side by side. The Captain here, he stands on his side an' calls out fer their Captain, an' she steps up bold as brass in front of him. An' she aint no looker either, I mean she might have been once, but now 'er nose is bent, and her face is scared all over. Now Blackbeard looks 'er right in the eye, pulls out 'is cutlass an' offers 'er a dual, all fair an' pirate like. In reply she lets out a banshee's wail and it's as if her ships grown guns strait out of 'er keel! Blackbeard knows she 'as 'im 'an she knows he 'as 'er. So they come to an accord, she takes 'er crews life an' he takes a new wife!"

At that the tavern bursts into raucous cheering and laughter. Call after call rings out toasting to Blackbeard's wife.

He slides back into his shadows, rage boiling up from his guts. He knows that ship, it's his ship. And he knows the Captain, for she's his too. Her broken nose and every last scar on her pretty little face were his gifts to her.

Well now he knew where to look for her, he intended to take back all that was rightfully his. Ned Low finished his drink and smiled. Now he knew where the whore who had wrecked his life and stole his ship sailed, he was going to hunt her down and finish what he had started. And if her bitch crew thought they could stop him, well let's see how they liked it when he gifted them to his new crew.

*End of book one.*

Printed in Great Britain
by Amazon

84201356R00149